Guilty

Guilty

Georges Bataille

Translated by Bruce Boone
Introduction by Denis Hollier

The Lapis Press

Le Coupable by Georges Bataille
© Editions Gallimard, 1961
English translation copyright © 1988 by Bruce Boone

Translator's Dedication:
To Ann Smock, thanks for friendship and help.

Thanks to Lee Hildreth and Steve Abbott for introducing me to
Bataille way back when; Bataille expert Denis Hollier for always
being on call to answer my questions; Stephen Mark for helping me
with Chapter One: Nighttime; Robert Glück for arranging for a
publisher when the book was in the planning stages and for a
valuable reading of the manuscript as a whole; Jaime Robles, my
editor at The Lapis Press, for constant friendly advice and help over
two years; Michael Taylor for a much-appreciated fine tuning of the
final draft; and most of all Ann Smock. Without her line-by-line
checking of my translations against the French originals, I would
often have been tempted to agree that Bataille really is as
untranslatable as they say. Thanks.

Earlier versions of some of these chapters appeared in *Temblor*,
Ottotole, *Mirage*, and *LAICA Journal*.

Cover photograph courtesy of Instituto di Anatomia e Istologia
Patologica, University of Florence, Italy.

The Lapis Press
589 N. Venice Blvd.
Venice CA 90291

ISBN 0-932499-60-0 Paper
ISBN 0-932499-55-4 Cloth

CONTENTS

A Tale of Unsatisfied Desire
Introduction by Denis Hollier

At the beginning of *Inner Experience*, Bataille conjures up the "laudable project of writing a book." *Guilty* isn't actually a book, and if it's
a collection of notes jotted from day to day, it isn't what is convention-
ally known as a journal either. Rather, it's an experimental document:
a record of involvement, or of meditation and illumination practices,
as these devolved in the confines of non-religious mysticism, and of various meditation techniques—a registering and rapid transcribing, while
they are taking place, of experiences whose waves or turbulence Bataille
felt in the course of the war years.

Bataille, a prolific writer, showed, with regard to his book, an odd
sense of neglect. The shorthand of *Guilty* corresponds with something
infinitely more urgent than the project (however laudable this might be)
of writing a book. Bataille isn't concerned with giving thoughts a systematic form or developing a story. He doesn't attempt to demonstrate,
convince, or impose—he notes, transcribes immediately, without hesi-
tation, an experience as elusive as it is urgent, as imperious as ungraspable ("fingers that don't grasp," he says). If by "writer" what is understood is simply a man who turns out books, there's no place for Bataille
in the category of writers. Still, the vigor of his often anxious (but rarely
insolent) indifference to literature makes his writing a major twentieth
century speech event—a stifled and jagged voice is struggling in the lab-
yrinth of language.

(Syntax has rarely been stretched to such an extreme point, been so
rarefied, eroded, exhausted, made light from within, buoyed up along
a set of suspension points and along such airy cushioning. There's a
kind of never-falling phrasal levitation—cadences with no resolution.

Violent expenditures of energy infrequently characterize a "good" writer. Can writing be good if it means harm? If it doesn't mean well?)

"The date I start (September 5, 1939) is no coincidence." *Guilty* isn't what people mean by a war book. The experience it transcribes is no less linked, in a strange and essential way, to events. For Sartre, the war occasioned a conversion to militant seriousness, the participation in a heroic performance. For Bataille, a (for some, shocking) feeling of lightness accompanied it. He doesn't *make* but *lives* war. There's nothing military, nothing activist in him. "Heroism," he notes, "is an attitude of escapism." War, an important way of "not-knowing" the future, is first a suspension of every plan. This anguished, anguishing catalyst dooms human existence to an irremediable and labyrinthine disorientation, to the glorious intoxication which is the incompleteness of all human life. It isn't that he takes war lightly—it's that war takes him lightly. Bataille no longer speaks of revolution, which is the will to attach meaning to laceration. In war, the law of struggle is displayed in its nakedness, and ontological discord asserts the radicalness of nonmeaning. Being's unbearable lightness: war is a name for what, elsewhere, Bataille terms torment.* "War professionals, so called," he writes, "are unfamiliar with these feelings. War is an activity that answers their needs. They go to the front to avoid anguish."

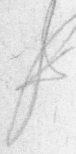

Why this title, *Guilty*? Bataille often puts the word in quotes, as if showing citation or a borrowing. He refers in fact to the world of Kafka (whose name appears several times). Bataille's lightness in living the war suggests K.'s indifference in *The Trial*—the way K. overlooks even his most pressing responsibilities. We don't know what the initial indictment was, but the behavior of the defendant makes up for this by substituting an unmistakable and unrepentant refusal to help anyone (himself) in danger. K. wastes his time with childishness (Bataille's word for it in his chapter on Kafka in *Literature and Evil*). He doesn't take his troubles seriously enough or, rather, forgets them, less interested in his lawyers' vanity than in their secretaries' sex appeal. He doesn't take himself sufficiently seriously.

The notes that make up *Guilty* show Bataille prey to the same methodical distraction. Guilty: "As I approached the summit...everything

* See Bataille's November 21, 1939 "Discussion of War" (with Koryé, Landsberg, Moré, and Wahl. *Digraphe*, 17, December 1978, p. 127.) "Today," he says, "I want to show what is most human—perhaps even what is the summit of the human mind—in this apparently insupportable situation. The fact of the uncertainty in which we live clarifies more than obscures, perhaps, the nature of things. I'm inclined to show how man ventures to fulfill himself when he accepts the incompletion of all things in which he lives, no longer seeing in them a point of reference but a motive of glory."

got confused. At the decisive moment there's always something else to do." Guilty: "Start out...forget it...don't conclude. As far as I'm concerned that's the right method and the only one able to deal with objects that resemble *it*." Guilty: "I've often thought that at the summit of existence there could be only insignificance." Guilty: "Blouses undone, afternoon laughter, the sun shines down on me with deadly laughter, rousing a wasp's stinger in me...."

A ladybug lights on a sheet of paper on which Bataille outlined (probably during one of Kojève's classes) the architecture of the Hegelian system. The bug goes strolling from chapter to chapter, from category to category. Elsewhere, a train pulls into a station. What does this mean? These accidental events are so many wounds inflicted on the system. They subvert any reaching of conclusions. In a completed world there would be no room left to notice such accidents. The subversive power of the anecdotal is such as to prevent the world from reaching completion. Bataille returns to this point several times—only in a completed universe are these trifles unable to retain their hold on our attention, do they have less weight than the system that completes the universe. Breaks in the narrative, like these, are inductors of incompleteness. Picking up on them, the seismograph which is *Guilty* registers light tremors of non-meaning.

(What happens—pure happiness—is insignificant. And philosophy will always prefer sadness, which at least means something or suffers in any case from not doing so. Philosophy speaks to a need for meaning, it respects it, it answers it. Sadness allows empathy, it can be understood and shared. We make sense and understand each other through it. Togetherness bathes in sadness. This is the keynote of every communion. Against Camus, Bataille once claimed that happiness can get along quite well without hope. There is nothing gregarious about pure happiness, which isn't ever divided up. The lesson found in the gay science urges that the truth of the trace is in the smile that effaces it, in the lightness of the laugh that dissolves it.)

The writing of the first sentence of *Guilty* was preceded for Bataille by ten years of planning. From the time of Surrealism on, he was active in avant-garde writing in Paris. He edited magazines (like *Documents* and *Acéphale*), took part in the activities of a number of political, or literary, or political and literary groups like Boris Souvarine's Democratic Communist Circle, *Contre-Attaque*, and (just before the war broke out) the College of Sociology. From this busy, prolific, and intense era, there remain numerous articles, manifestoes and lectures that comprise the first two volumes of the *Complete Works*—a thousand pages giving testimony to an amazing lucidity, boldness, and ability to provoke. But oddly, no book. These texts, forgotten by the author himself for more than thirty years, in magazines that were themselves forgotten, would be rediscovered only after his death.

Bataille suffered from lack of recognition. The dynamic and influential thinking of the last twenty years owes so much to him (and paradoxically owes so much of its influence to him) that we ourselves find it difficult to believe in that lack. The aesthetics of formlessness developed in the articles in *Documents*, the general economy contained in the notion of expenditure, the interpretation of Fascism he developed in 1933, all had their readers, though few. For Bataille, the College of Sociology was an attempt to go beyond this isolation and to acquire recognition for the seriousness of his thought. He believed that by putting his ideas forward systematically he would impose a respect for the notions around which his system and obsessions revolved (the ambiguity of sacredness as the focus simultaneously of attraction and repulsion, the wagering of the subject in experience, and the sacrificial aspect of knowledge). The war came, though. At that level too it ended the planning. Bataille hoped, through the College of Sociology, for some of the recognition that so far had eluded him. But with the outbreak of war, he turned his mind elsewhere.

Bataille was 42 when, on September 5, 1939, he jotted down in his notebook the first line of what would become *Guilty*. The difference between *Guilty* and his pre-war texts can be described in topographical (or geographical) terms. The latter texts had certainly been Parisian—they were linked to the intellectual life of the avant-garde, to its discoveries, enthusiasms, and quarrels. On the other hand, the majority of the notebooks that made up *Guilty* were composed in the country. Bataille, ill with tuberculosis, had taken time off from his job and moved to Vézelay. In rapidly sketched phrases, a regular rhythm opens up a landscape—hills, clouds, movements of the sun, nights, the sky—and constitutes an aspect of Bataille's experience that gives his mysticism a romantic, rustic tone. But the difference of place can be described in still other terms. Bataille's pre-war efforts took the form of open letters, lectures, pamphlets or manifestoes, texts addressing an *audience*—and very much so, their second person often being in the imperative. The notes comprising *Guilty* have a far more complex strategy of communication, and their destination remains less legible.

The manifesto written for the College of Sociology was titled "The Sorcerer's Apprentice." It starts with a theorem: "An absence of need is more unfortunate than an absence of satisfaction." Kojève, the charismatic commentator on Hegel, had described the impasses of desire as it seeks recognition—a desire, he claims, in which the definition of mankind can be seen. Desire, that is to say non-satisfaction (desire and not its satisfaction), is that by which mankind affirms itself, distinguishes itself from animal life. In the appendix of *Guilty* Bataille inserted a letter written to Kojève after a lecture of his at the College of Sociology. Going over it again five years later, he alters its impact appreciably in a way that clarifies the breach that the war occasioned. In the longer first draft, Bataille's departure point is Kojève's hypothesis concerning the end of history:* Man has nothing more to do, he has in a certain way already fulfilled his destiny, and history is now over, "except for the wrap-up." What will he do now with his freedom, now that there's no use for it, now that there's nothing left to deny, nothing else to transform? The first draft of the letter represents an optimistic response—the only thing man can do with this freedom, which is now without a job, is to bring about recognition of it. When the time to transform the world has passed, when political and technical action have fulfilled their historic task, the negation of the world seeks—beyond art or religion—non-productive forms. The Popular Front had lobbied for a decreased workday and had taken strong stands on leisure. Bataille outlines a populist version of his notion of expenditure—the new agenda of "utilization of leisure time" opens up a field where recognition of "unused negativity" will be sought. The second version of the letter, the one that figures in *Guilty*, is, however, much less positive. In it Bataille edits out everything that, in terms of a desire for recognition, suggests finding any satisfaction. Recognition of unused negativity is now precluded—as is satisfaction of a desire for recognition. The experience of (desire's) negativity is linked to radical solitude. "In fact no one," he writes to Blank, "could 'recognize' a summit that would be night. Several facts (like the extraordinary difficulty I experience in getting 'recognized' at the simple level at which others are 'recognized') led me to take the hypothesis of 'irrevocable insignificance' seriously, but cheerfully."

With Paris behind Bataille, was what Kojève described as the struggle for recognition behind him too? *Guilty* is the simultaneously distracted and rigorous transcription, communication, and recognition of what isn't recognizable. The unimportance, the insignificance of what is recognizable. The experience of what's lost in communicating. "These notes link me to my fellow humans as a guideline, and everything else seems empty to me, though I wouldn't have wanted friends reading them." Sartre would soon associate the experience of shame with the

* This appears in *The College of Sociology* (1937-1939), University of Minnesota Press, 1988.

feeling a subject has when exposed to the gaze of another. Bataille here associates friendship and guilt quite closely. I recognize my friends by the shame I feel at the idea that they'll read what I write.* A person's only friends are tactless ones—I'm ashamed as I picture them reading what I write. Shame comes to writing from the fact that friends will read what I haven't written for them.

Probably it was Bataille who in 1953 wanted to give the English translation of *Histoire de l'oeil/Story of the Eye* a title associated with a Blake poem—"A Tale of Satisfied Desire." Ten years earlier he quoted the poem in *Guilty* (a section of which is entitled "Gratified Desire"): "In a wife I would desire / What in whores is always found / The lineaments of Gratified Desire." (He'll cite it again in the essay on Blake in *Literature and Evil.*) This isn't the desire of desire but of satisfaction. But a desire for this satisfaction, formulated in the conditional, isn't ever satisfied itself. And throughout the course of *Guilty*, Bataille more often suggests the horror of being satisfied, the horror of satisfaction, than the delights of satisfied desire: "Desire desires *not* to be satisfied." True desire is a desire for desire, not satisfaction. It always stages the emptiness of satisfaction.

In Bataille, eroticism doesn't accompany a fullness of sexual communion. Non-satisfaction is pivotal. First of all, sex is an experience of what separates people. "I know satisfaction doesn't satisfy us." The sentences of *Guilty* are often incomplete, have ("incomplete successes") the beauty of ruins, chant a hymn to incompletion, one that culminates in a final alleluia—a stifled version of the *Canticle of Canticles.* At this point the two appendixes of *Guilty* join the Kojève letter and *The Alleluia.*

·

Guilty is the first Bataille book I acquired. An erroneous quotation from a reader's guide to existentialism (whose author was a Jesuit, I was told) had caught my attention—"I teach turning anguish to delirium." Years later I would discover this was a typo. French makes "delirium" (*délire*) closer to "delights" (*délice*) than English does. Luckily, I was at an age when "delirium" has greater impact than "delight." *Inner Experience*, from which the quotation was drawn, wasn't on the shelves of any bookstore I could find. One of them, though, had *Guilty*—by the same author. I felt I was buying an old book, one from another time.

* For this poetics of guilt in Bataille, see my "Bataille's Tomb: A Halloween Story" (*October*, no. 33 [Summer 1985]).

Between that purchase and the publication, however, only fifteen years had elapsed. Bataille was still living. It was thirty years ago.

At about the same time I spent a few days on a farm (in Auvergne) whose feudal tower the new proprietor wanted to renovate. The previous owner, a relative of his, had just died, I think. Books lay around the different rooms, indicating she had been a cultivated woman—classics, half a century of prize-winning works. What had put *Guilty* in that collection? I never found out. The closest city to the hamlet was Billom. I later would learn that Bataille was born there. He visited the town during the 1940 mass exodus and several fragments from *Guilty* were written there. No other book has given me such an impression of being impregnated with war atmosphere, the weather of wartime.

Guilty

...with a shot of gin
a night of rowdiness
stars fall from the sky

Drinking heavily from sky's thunder
heart shattered by lightning
I burst into laughter

Introduction

To introduce the first edition of *Guilty*,* I wrote these words, whose general meaning related to an impression I had in 1942—that I lived in the world like a stranger. (In a way this didn't surprise me—more often than we suspect, Kafka's dreams in their various guises express the reality of things...):

> *Someone who called himself Dianus† wrote these notes and died.*
> *He (ironically?) thought of himself as guilty.*
> *The collection appearing under this name is a completed work.*
> *A letter together with fragments of a work recently begun comprise*
> *its appendix.*

.

It isn't my purpose in these few lines—which introduce the republication of my first two books‡—to try to discover the principle these reflections issued from...but to say more modestly how...from my point of view...my way of thinking diverges from others'. Especially from the way of thinking of philosophers. Mostly it diverges on account of my ineptitude. The requisite knowledge didn't come to me till late in life. I was told I was really gifted and I should...Critical reviews though—

---

* Gallimard, 1944.
† I used the pseudonym Dianus (from Roman mythology) when I first published these opening pages of *Guilty* in the April 1940 issue of *Mesures*, the issue printed in Abbeville.
‡ *L'Expérience intérieure*, 2nd rev. ed., followed by *Méthode de Méditation*, 1954; *Le Coupable* [*Guilty*], 2nd rev. ed., followed by *L'Alleluiah*. These two books comprise volumes I and II of *La Somme athéologique* (Gallimard).

I'm talking about criticism that had to do with the first volume of this work, and there wasn't any dearth of it—left me cold. (I have other, possibly more reasonable, worries....)

Today I'd like to propose the reason my thinking diverged so strongly from the thinking of others: *I'm afraid*. I never considered that my job was to reveal truth day by day more clearly. I think like a person who's sick, someone who can't get his breath, is flattened. Fear carries me onward. Fear or horror, of the stakes involved in systematic thought.

The search for truth isn't my strong point (mainly I mean the phrases expressing it). But this is the issue I have to consider now: that, more than the truth, it's fear I'm after. Fear opened by a dizzying fall. Fear reached by possibly unlimited movements of thought.

It seemed to me there were two terms to human thought: God and the awareness of God's absence. But since God's just a confusion of the SACRED (a religious aspect) and REASON (an instrumental aspect), the only place for him is a world where confusion of the instrumental and the sacred becomes a basis for reassurance. God terrifies when he's no longer the same as reason (Pascal and Kierkegaard). But if he's not the same as reason, I'm confronted with God's absence. And this absence is confused with the last stage of the world, which no longer has anything instrumental about it and furthermore doesn't have anything to do with *future* retributions or punishment. So the question still is outstanding....

> —...*fear...yes, fear, that only boundless thought can reach*...fear, yes, but what *of*...?
> The answer fills the universe and the universe in me:
> —...very clearly, of NOTHING....

.

Clearly, I'm bound to tremble if the object of my fear isn't limited by reason. I have to tremble if the possibility of gambling doesn't attract me.

But humanly speaking, since any gamble remains by definition open, it's bound in the long run to lose....

Gambling doesn't call into question just the material results created by work but the same results as the outcome of play without work. Play or fortune. On the battlefield luck gets confused with courage or strength, but in the last analysis these are forms of chance. If forms of chance can accommodate work, then work loses at least something of its pure form. This doesn't detract from the truth that work, when it makes its own contribution, increases the gambler's chances. It does this to the degree that (in an appropriate way) gambling is also work.

But in the last analysis, work's accommodation with play leaves work the advantage. The contribution of work to play finally yields completely to work, and then play has the diminished place of inevitability.

So that even if temperament hadn't yielded me to anguish, the roads opened up by play wouldn't be a solid option. Play leads finally only to anguish. And our only possibility is work.

Anguish isn't really a possibility for us. Naturally not! Anguish is *im*-possibility! In the sense that the impossible defines me. Mankind is the only animal that knows just how—heavily—to make its own death an impossibility, since we're the only animal to die in this constricted sense. Consciousness is the condition of a death that's *achieved*. I die to the degree I'm aware of dying. And as death takes my consciousness away from me, I'm not just aware that I'm dying: death is also taking away this awareness....

Maybe humankind's a pinnacle, but only a disastrous one.
Like a delirium of sunset, the dying person sinks into a magnificence that escapes him and escapes to the degree that it enlarges him. In that instant tears start to laugh, laughter weeps. And time?...Time reaches a simplicity that cancels it.

·

To be honest, the language I'm using can't be complete until my death. Provided that death isn't confused with the violent, theatrical form chance gives it. Death is a disappearance. It's a suppression so perfect that at the pinnacle utter silence is its truth. Words can't describe it. Here obviously I'm summoning a silence I can only approach from the outside or from a long way away.

I'll add this. If I died right now, the unbearable pain of it would be added to my life. My suffering—which would conceivably make my death more painful to my survivors—wouldn't change the fact that I'd been suppressed.

This is how I finally reach the end of language, which is death. Potentially the question's still one of language, but the meaning of this language (already meaning's absence) is implicit in words that put a stop to language. But these words acquire meaning only to the extent they take place immediately before silence—a silence that puts a stop to them. Only *forgotten* would they take on full meaning, falling suddenly, conclusively, into oblivion.

In any case, silence is the only border we can reach in the realm you and I dwell in. Even the equivocal silence of ecstasy itself isn't attainable, if it comes to that. Or like death it's attainable for a moment.

Will I let my thought slowly and slyly (cheating as little as possible) devolve into silence?*

---

* No. Not yet! The job of comparing my thought with the thought of others would still remain. With everyone's? Possibly. I'm getting to a foregone conclusion. Is systematic thought forever beyond us (as it was in one way or another for Hegel, who in a sense died drowning...)?

FRIENDS

1 Nighttime

The date I start (September 5, 1939) is no coincidence. I'm starting because of what's happening, though I don't want to go into it. I'm writing it down because of being unable *not* to. From now on I have to respond to impulses of freedom and whims. No more evasions! I have to say things straight out....

It's so impossible to read—most books anyway. I've lost the urge. What's depressing is the amount of work I have to do. I'm always on edge, I get drunk often. I'm true to life if I eat and drink what I want. Life's a delight, a feast, a celebration, it's an incomprehensible and oppressive dream with charms I'm hardly blind to. Being conscious of chance lets me see a difficult fate for what it is. And chance wouldn't stand a chance if it weren't for sheer craziness.

On a crowded train standing up, I began reading Angela de Foligno's *Book of Visions*.

I'm copying it out, uncontrollably excited—the veil's torn in two and I'm emerging from my fog of flailing impotence. The Holy Ghost speaks to the Saint, "I'll speak to you all along your way. There won't be any interruption in the flow of my words and I defy you to listen to anyone else's, since I've bound you to me and won't release you till you've come here again. And then I'll only free you relatively—relative to this joy today. But relative to everything else, never never—if you love me." The next few pages express a love so rapturous only torment could fuel it. I live like a pig according to Christians, but that's a ridiculous thought I don't want to stop with. The cause of my thirst is the desire I have to burn up. I suffer from not being like *her* and coming near death, coming to close quarters with death and inhaling it like a lover's breath.

Everything takes place in a fiery penumbra, its meaning subtly withdrawn. The earth lies prey to some incomprehensible wrong. Something silent, fugitive, exasperating, exalting.

What sneaky weather. A muffled sound of air-raid sirens (in the little valley of F, with a forest at the skyline and, above it, a haziness—there's a funny wailing sound of a factory set among ancient trees and houses). A nightmare is my truth and nakedness. The logical thread inserted into this is so ridiculous! I like to wrap myself up in reality's vagueness, in misty sheets where I cuddle at the center of a new world I'm now a part of. Unbearable stench of fog (making me feel like bursting into screams...). I'm all by myself, drowned in a rising tide of euphoria which is within me, that sees its own value and is gentle like ocean waves. At night in bed I'm awash with the immense light of night, drunk with lucid anguish. As long as I know how pointless things are, I can stand it. No one relates to the war madness, I'm the only one who can do this. Others don't love life with such anguished drunkenness: in the shadow of bad dreams, they don't recognize *themselves*. They're unaware of the roads sleepwalkers set out on, going from contented laughter to hopeless excitement.

I won't speak of war, but of mystical experience. I'm not unaffected by the war. I'd be glad to give my blood, weariness, and what's more, the brutal moments undergone at death's approach.... But how even for a moment can I dismiss this non-knowledge, a feeling of having lost my way in some underground tunnel? To me this world, the planet, the starry sky, are just a grave (I don't know if I'm suffocating here, if I'm crying or becoming some kind of incomprehensible sun). Even war can't light up a darkness that is this total.

Desire for a woman's body, for a tender, erotically naked woman (she's wearing perfume, she has kinky jewelry on). When I'm feeling such pangs of lust, I know best what I am. A sort of hallucinatory darkness pushes me slowly over the edge towards craziness and I start twisting towards impossibility. Towards who knows what hot, flowery, fatal explosion...in which I escape the illusion of any solid connection between me and the world. My true church is a whorehouse—the only one that gives me true satisfaction. I earnestly try to find out what makes saints so passionate and intense, but their "requiescats" are too final for my unholy light-heartedness. I've had my own peaceful ecstasies and insights; a half-glimpsed realm that, even if it could give me stability, I'd end up cursing, even if this meant being banished.

Mystical and erotic experience differ in that the former is totally successful. Erotic licentiousness results in depression, disgust, and the inability to continue. Unsatisfied sexual need completes suffering. Eroticism's too heavy a burden for human strength. The torment of orgies is inseparable from the agony of war as Jünger pictured it: in the morning you wake up under the table with the litter of the previous evening around you. This is a *given* for orgies, a condition without which they wouldn't exist.

The one I was at (took part in it) last night was as crude as you might imagine. I followed the example of the worst, out of simplicity. In the middle of an uproar, of falling bodies, I'm silent and affectionate, not hostile. To me, the sight's horrible (but more horrible still are the rationalizations and tricks people resort to to protect themselves from such disgusting things, to distance themselves from their inevitable needs).

Blameless, shameless. The more desperate the eroticism, the more hopelessly women show off their heavy breasts, opening their mouths and screaming out, the greater the attraction. In contrast, a promise of light awaits at the limits of the mystical outlook. I find this unbearable and soon return to insolence and erotic vomit—which doesn't respect anybody or anything. How sweet to enter filthy night and proudly wrap myself in it. The whore I went with was as uncomplicated as a child and she hardly talked. There was another one, who came crashing down from a tabletop—sweet, shy, heartbreakingly tender, as I watched her with drunken, unfeeling eyes.

Unlike political men, a god doesn't bother with how things are. For a god, they just *are* whatever they are, war or prostitution—not good and not bad, only divine.

The gods are utterly indifferent to (their own) motivations, which are so deep there's no equivalent in our language.

Godhead (in the sense of "godlike" not "of God," that slavish creator and physician of mankind), force, power, drunkenness, ecstasy, the joy of not existing any more, "dying from not dying." And this all my life: the womanish impulses of my heart. The other aspect is the dryness, the unquenchable thirst, the unconquerable cold.

I hope the heavens are ripped open (the moment when the intelligible disposition of objects, which though known have become alien, yields to a presence that is intelligible only to the heart). This I hoped for, but the skies never opened. There's a mystery in my crouching here like a beast of prey, flesh gripped by hunger. It's completely absurd: "Is God the animal I'd like to tear apart?" As if I was *really* a beast of prey. But I'm sicker than that. My hunger holds no interest for me. Rather than eat, my desire is to be eaten. Love eats my living bones, and the only *release* is quick death. I'm waiting for an answer from the dark in which I exist. What if it turned out that instead of being ground to pieces, I was just forgotten about, like some kind of waste? There isn't an answer in all this flailing about. Just emptiness. Now say that.... There's no *God*, though, for me to get down on my knees to.

I'm going to say this as straightforwardly as I can. If people think of my life as a sickness to be cured only by God, they should just keep quiet for a minute. And if they then discover real silence, I'm asking them not to be reluctant to back off. Because they haven't seen what they're talking about. In contrast with myself, who has seen *unintelligibility** face to face and has burned with love that can't be imagined as being greater. I saw. Slowly and *happily*. I couldn't stop laughing. The burden (pacifying slavishness that commences as soon as you start talking about God) lifted from my shoulders. A wrenching vision of *unintelligibility* (steeped in death and transfigured by it—but glorious) is set before the world of living beings; but at the same time we're offered the temptation of theology's ordered vision. Once you realize you've been abandoned and that your vanity has been rendered helpless between the absence of a solution and the banal answer of the mysteries of a self, there's nothing left in you but a wound.

For if in the final analysis some immutable satisfaction does exist, why am I rejected? But I *know* satisfaction doesn't satisfy us and that humankind's glory is its awareness of not knowing anything but glory

---

* By "unintelligibility" I don't mean God. I mean what's felt by us when, following those who use the word God and the beliefs associated with the word, we discover we're in a state of confusion, one that makes little children go looking for their mothers. In *real* loneliness, an *illusion* corresponds to the believer and *unintelligibility* to the non-believer. [1960 Note]

and non-satisfaction. Someday my tragedy will know completion and I'll die. Only that day, because I've anticipated it and put myself in its light, gives meaning to what I am. I haven't any other hope. Joy, love, a relaxed freedom, these are bound up with my hatred of satisfaction.

It's as if there's a crab in my head. A crab, a toad, some horror I have to puke up, no matter what.

At this time of dark impossibility my only possibilities are drunkenness, promiscuity, combat. Deep inside, everything's scrunched up. The idea I have is to put up with these horrible things and endure them, without giving in to the tugs of the vertigo.

I have some idea about the reasons for my lack of goodwill. I'm as unwilling as anyone to reject the hopelessness of a given situation. I've always tried to protect myself from threats of possibility. When daylight threatened, sleep calmed me. This is the limit that comes into the picture if I want to act and if I try to open up the secrets of the inner world. A decisive passion, an accidental irruption occurs now and then. Torpor follows like an immovable sphinx deaf to the questions asked, eyes empty, absorbed in its own enigma. I realize now that this alternation paralyzes me. But I love the animal wisdom of this state—capricious, it's more sure of itself than any other wisdom.

Prey to such paralysis, I spread my existence slowly through earth and sky. As the phrase goes, I'm "the tree with roots that delve deep into the earth": I'm as tough as I am slow. At times I accept a necessity of a feeling of dark binding growth, of building up strength. The growing strength balances my awareness of increased fragility.

I wanted to accept the responsibility for this, myself. Sitting on the edge of the bed, facing a window and the night, I practiced, determined to become a war zone myself. The urge to sacrifice and the urge to be sacrificed meshed like gears when a drive-shaft starts up and the teeth interlock.

What's called *substance* is just a provisional equilibrium between the spending (loss) and the accumulation of force. *Stability* can never exceed this short-lived, relative equilibrium; to my mind, it's not and can't ever be static. Life itself is linked to these states of equilibrium, although relative equilibrium signifies only that life is possible. But this doesn't mean that life's not an accumulation and loss of force. It's a constant destabilization of the equilibrium without which it wouldn't be. There's no such thing as discrete substance, for only the universe can possess what's called substance. But we understand substance as something that tends towards unity, and unity as tending towards a system of condensation/explosion in which duration is excluded. So what characterizes the universe appears to be a different kind of thing than substance is: since substance is only a precarious quality whose appearance is associated with individual beings. The universe is no more reducible to that lazy notion of substance than it is to outbursts of laughter or kisses. Outbursts of laughter and kisses won't produce notions, and they attain "what is" more truly than ideas with which objects are manipulated. What could be more ridiculous than reducing "what is"—the universe, if you like—to analogies with useful objects! Laughter, lovemaking, even tears of rage and of my own impotence in knowing, these are means of knowing that can't be located on a plane of intelligence. The most that can be said is that they compromise with intelligence, so that intelligence then assimilates laughter or love-making or tears to the other modes of action and to the reaction of objects among themselves. These modes appear first in the intelligence like subordinated aspects of reality. For all that, laughter and other non-productive emotions are no less able to reduce intelligence to infirmity. Intelligence becomes conscious of its misery, though we can't in any way confound two experiences of the universe that are irreducible to each other. Only confusion and subordination allow us to speak of God. God the slave demands my enslavement to the second power in order to multiply chains endlessly. Laughing at the universe liberated my life. I escape its weight by laughing. I refuse any intellectual translations of this laughter, since my slavery would commence from that point on.

We have to go beyond.

"Where I was, I was looking for love and couldn't find it. I even lost the love I'd brought along with me till then, and I became non-love." (*Book of Visions*, 23.)

When Angela de Foligno speaks of God she speaks like a slave. But what she expresses has the power to shake me. I stammer. And the saint's words are another instance of stammering. I won't dwell on what might be construed as the reflection of time's arrangement of the states of things—chains which today are broken (though reforged in other ways).

She continues:

"...When God appears in the dark, there's no laughter or ardor or devotion or love, there's nothing on your face or in your heart, not a shudder, not a movement. The body sees nothing, the eyes of the soul open up. The body rests and sleeps, stays speechless and motionless. All the acts of friendship God has vouchsafed me, numerous and indescribable, and his sweetnesses and gifts and words and operations, all this is small when placed next to Him whom I see in the vastness of the dark."

If the laughter is violent enough, there'll be no limiting it.

These notes link me to my fellow humans as a guideline, and everything else seems empty to me, though I wouldn't have wanted friends reading them. The result is I have the impression of writing from the grave. I'd like them to be published when I'm dead...only there's the possibility I'll live a long time, and publication will be in my lifetime. The idea makes me suffer. I might change. But I have a feeling of anguish meantime.*

What could be pleasanter or more innocent than my conversation with two hookers? Naked as she-wolves in a forest of mirrors and colored lights. People with moral standards naively think of me as "wild."

* Actually, I was to give fragments of this text to the magazine *Mesures* at the start of 1940 (under the pseudonym Dianus). Coming back from my exodus, I learned there were copies of *Mesures* in the Abbeville town depot, kept there during the battle for the North, and since the town had been quite heavily bombed I thought the chances of publication were remote for some time. The *Mesures* issue was intact though. In 1943 *L'Expérience intérieure* was published. The first edition of *Guilty* was to appear at the beginning of 1944, in February. [1960 Note]

2 Gratified Desire

In a wife I would desire
What in whores is always found
The lineaments of Gratified Desire
WILLIAM BLAKE

I'm writing, happy that some occasion has afforded me satisfaction. Again I imagine an approach—a possible life—without pre-given notions.

Sharp serenity, the sky before me black, star-filled, the hill black and so too the trees: I've found out why my heart's a banked fire, though inside still alive. There's a feeling of presence in me irreducible to any kind of notion—the thunderbolt that ecstasy causes. I become a towering flight from myself as if my life flowed in slow rivers through the inky sky. I've stopped being ME. But whatever issues from me reaches and encloses boundless presence, itself similar to the loss of myself, which is no longer either myself or someone else. And a deep kiss between us, in which the distinction of our lips is lost, is linked to that ecstasy and is dark, familiar to the universe as the earth wheeling through heaven's loss.

The Sacrifice can begin at that instant. At that instant Non-satisfaction, Wrath, and Pride recommence. In silence and charged with self-loathing, a crow awkward as it flies, burdened down with loathing even for itself, greedy to abolish what still is called Affection and Love; this ecstasy is intolerable now and what's left to subsist is an empty manliness. . . . . I'm alone. I see the garden rising up opposite me in the back, like the architecture of a vast funeral monument. It's open at my feet, so dark and deep it seems like a pit.

My description falters—maybe it's incomprehensible. I picture a man on his deathbed, wanting, by a sign, to bear witness to his life for one last time. The sign means something has taken place. But what? However, it's possible to follow what I'm saying, I think, and test it out (more thoroughly in the first part than in the second).

In staggering chaos. My thick peasant head resists it. Body blows from the alcohol leave me feeling only "satisfied desire." It's hard to see the mediocre inconsistency of my life in the mess of these lines. If power remains in me, I exhaust it by dealing with the vulgarity of circumstances, by being elusive, by wordlessly disengaging myself from what seems to confine me.

It's pleasant sometimes—even if I have to go out of my way to do this—to go past the Madeleine. From there I can just make out the Obelisque through the colonnades of Palais Gabriel and above the Palais Bourbon, its needle twinned by the gilded dome of Les Invalides. To me, the setting represents the tragedy a nation played out: royalty, key to the monumental architecture, toppled in blood—amid jeers from an angry crowd—and then born again in stony silence, circumspect and inscrutable to busy pedestrians glancing up as they hurry by. My breath quickens as I think of the "soul of the world" buried there, glorified in the architecture of Les Invalides. I easily evade what dazes simpler souls, but this Hegelian structure—fallen twice—finds faint echoes in me. Glory, disaster, and silence combined in ungraspable mystery, from the depths of which the Obelisque rises. Since the war twice I've come to the foot of the monolith—which I've never seen in this darkness. Failing a nighttime visit like this one, its utter majesty escapes you. From the base, I saw the granite block lost deep in the sky, the angles outlined on scatterings of stars. At night the lofty stone had the majesty of mountains—it was like death, like quiet sands, lovely as darkness, cracked like a drum-roll.

I intend a description of mystical experience and am apparently off the track, but in the confusion I introduce, what track *could* there be?

A naked body, shown off, can be seen without interest. Similarly, it's easy to look at the sky and see only emptiness. Still, a displayed body keeps, I think, the same power it has in sex play. And in a serene or brooding sky, I can open a wound that I'll cling to as to a woman's nudity. The cause of a man's psychological ecstasy, in sex with a woman, is delight in her coolness. So, too, in the emptiness of space and in open depths of the universe, the strangeness of this meditation reaches a cause that frees me.

I described what I felt this evening meditating on, looking at, a black cloud, whose displacement seemed "acrobatic" to me—its parts twisted and tangled.

I don't confuse my sexual licentiousness and my mystical life. The description of Tantrism in Eliade's book left me hostile. I don't like to mix my enthusiasms. In addition to being remote from the purposeful indifference of Tantrism, compromise attempts only succeeded in further alienating me from possibilities of this kind. I'll come back to them—later—intending to vouch for the wild state I associate with my own experience.

Shouting in the throes of passion, lost in widening depths around which lightning plays, can it really matter to us *what is* at the bottom of an abyss? Writing, I still feel flames, and refuse to go further. What could I add? I can't describe the wall of flame that opens in the sky— what is suddenly *there*, piercing and gentle and simple, unbearable as a child's death. Fear seizes me as I write these last words, fear of the empty silence I am when face to face with.... Determination is necessary if a person's to endure a light so blinding, if you're not to experience empty understanding. Determination not to become weak when a single truth is clear—that attempting to enclose *what's there* in intellectual categories is the same as being reduced to a proud inability to laugh, a result of faith in God. To remain a man in the light requires the courage of demented incomprehension; it means being set on fire, letting go with screams of joy, waiting for death, acting in a realization of some presence you don't and can't know. It means becoming love and blind light, yourself, and attaining the perfect incomprehension of the sun.

It's impossible to gain access to this manly incomprehension without grasping the secret of your desire for nakedness. First of all, we have to transgress prohibitions, a blind obeying of which is related to God's transcendence and our own humiliation.

Shattered humanity doesn't cease drifting along a river, which is deaf to all our words, when suddenly the sound of a waterfall looms in the distance....

The hard, luminous nudity of buttocks, the unquestionable truth of cliffs in a trough of sea and sky. In the period between the two world wars, alcohol was as necessary as lies. The absence of a solution can't be expressed.

3 Angel

In its cruelty, eroticism brings indigence, demands ruinous outlays. Moreover it's too expensive to be thought of in relation to asceticism. On the other hand, mystical and ecstatic states (which don't entail moral or material ruin) can't do without certain extremes against self. My experience with the latter of these as well as the former makes me aware of the contrasting effects the two kinds of excess have. To give up my sexual habits would mean I'd have to discover some other means of tormenting myself, though this torture would have to be as intoxicating as alcohol.

Picturing an ascetic face, burning eyes, prominent cheekbones depresses me as I start to think of myself. My blind father with his sunken eyes, his hungry bird's long nose, his screams of pain, soundless peals of laughter. I think I'd like to be like him! How can I avoid questioning that tangible gloom? And I'm trembling from—throughout childhood —having to have that distressing, unwillingly ascetic face in front of me!

As you encounter an inevitable fate, the first thing you experience is a moment of recoil, and out of debauchery and rapture I've found a path to austerity. This morning, the bare thought of asceticism revived me. I couldn't imagine anything more desirable, but now I can't entertain the same image without disgust. I'm not about to be hostile, though— hollow-eyed, emaciated. If that's my fate, I can't escape, though this doesn't mean putting up with it either.

Complete candor—that's my own recommendation for myself as the first stage of asceticism. Always changing and going from one state to another, first excited, then depressed; this prevents existence from having a content. The worst thing would be the flux of passionate emotion. I picture poverty finally as a cure.

I want to transcribe an image that describes (if badly) an ecstatic vision. "An angel appears in the sky, just a shimmering spot, having the depth and darkness of night and beauty of inner light. But quivering—almost imperceptibly—this angel raises his crystal sword and it breaks."

This angel is a "movement of worlds," and I can't just love him as if he were a being like other beings. He's the wound and hidden flaw that turns me into "shattering crystal." But although I can't love him like an angel or a distinct entity, what I've understood frees up a movement in me that gives me the desire to die, to stop existing.

It's degrading to reduce the pleasures of unhappiness (the more unhappy you are the more they increase) to trite literary conventions. When pleasure wears an ascetic's face, when self-torment is naive and innocent—what you're dealing with can be found in the sky or the night or the cold, but not in literary history.

"God," says Angela de Foligno, "gave his Son whom he loved a poverty such that there never has been nor will ever be a poor man like him. And yet it is his as a property. Substance is his possession and he has it beyond human speech. God made him poor all the same, as if substance wasn't his."

I'm discussing Christian virtues now: poverty, humility. That even for God unchangeable substance can't be the same as supreme satisfaction, that renunciation and death are a "beyond" necessary for the glory of Him *who is* eternal beatitude (and as well, for the glory of whoever possesses the illusory attribute of substance in any way); truths of this destructive order wouldn't have been nakedly available to the saint. Still, if ecstatic vision is a concern, they can't be avoided.

Christianity's impoverishment lies in its will (through asceticism) to escape a state in which fragility or non-substance is painful. However, Christianity still has to make a *sacrifice* of substance, a necessity it asserts with difficulty.

A being that isn't cracked isn't possible. But we go from enduring the cracks (from decline) to glory (we seek out the cracks).

Christianity attains glory by escaping from what is (humanly) glorious. It has first of all to conceive of protecting what (compared with the fragility of things of this world) is substantial. Then God's sacrifice becomes possible, and the necessity of it comes into play immediately. In this way Christianity is the adequate expression of the human condition, and humanity can only enter sacrificial glory when no longer encumbered with the state of malaise in which instability left it. But this stage is faint-hearted. It's like people who can't bear letting go in (either an "erotic" or an "alcoholic") drunkenness. Christianity is left behind at the stage of exuberance. Angela de Foligno attained and described it, not realizing it.

There's the universe—and in the dead of its night, you discover its parts and in doing so discover yourself. When a person dies, his or her survivors are doomed to dismantle whatever that person believed in, to profane what he, she respected. I came to see the universe in a certain way, but inevitably future generations will see what was wrong. Completeness should be the basis of human knowledge. If it isn't complete, it's not *knowledge*—it's only an inevitable, giddy product of the will to know.

It was Hegel's greatness to see that knowledge depends on completeness (as if there could be knowledge worthy of the name while still in process!). Now, of the edifice he wanted to leave behind, there remains but an outline of the part constructed prior to his time (the outline wasn't established before or after him). Necessarily the outline that is the *Phenomenology of Mind* is in spite of everything only a beginning, a decisive failure. Completed knowledge occurs only when I say of human existence that it's a beginning that will never be completed. If this existence reached its possible limit, it wouldn't find any satisfaction; it wouldn't in any event satisfy the exigencies that are ours as living beings. It might define these exigencies as false, from the viewpoint of a truth that's half asleep. But judged by its own criteria, this is a truth on only one condition—that I die, and with me, whatever's incomplete about man. If my suffering were eliminated—if the incompletion of things stopped destroying our adequacy—human life would peter out. And as life vanished, so too would our far-off, inevitable truth, the truth that incompleteness, death, and unquenchable desire are, in a sense, being's never-to-be-healed wound, without which inertia (while death absorbs us into itself and there's no more change) would imprison us.

At the limits of reflection, the value of knowledge, it seems, depends on its ability to make any conclusive image of the universe impossible. Knowledge destroys fixed notions and this continuing destruction is its greatness, or more precisely, its truth. From the dark of illusory appearances, the movement of knowledge releases images stripped of existence. And avid for knowledge, confronting a constantly escaping possibility of knowing, the being I refer to remains finally, in its knowing non-knowledge, something like the unexpected result of this operation. The issue raised was *being* and *substance*, and what appears immediately (which results in the fact that the "essence of worlds" opens before me while I'm writing and that there stops being any difference inside me between knowledge and ecstatic "loss of knowledge")—what appears is that precisely where knowledge has searched for being it has found it incomplete. There's an identity of subject and object (the known object, the knowing subject) if incomplete and incompletable knowledge admits that the object, incomplete itself, is also "incompletable." Then the feeling of discomfort, brought on by the necessity which "incompletion" (humankind) feels it's under to discover "completion" (God), gets dispersed. Not to know the future (the *Unwissenheit um die Zukunft** which Nietzsche loved) is the final state of knowledge, and humanness becomes the type of an occurence that adequately (and so, inadequately) stands for an incompletion of worlds.

Describing incompleteness I found intellectual fullness and ecstasy coinciding, something I hadn't attained till then. I'm indifferent myself to the possibility of arriving at the Hegelian position—a suppression of the difference between (a known) object and (a knowing) subject, though this position corresponds to a fundamental difficulty. On the steep slope I'm climbing I now see truth as founded on incompletion (just as Hegel founded it on completion), though the "founding" in question is only an appearance! I've renounced what humankind thirsted for. I see that—gloriously—I'm elevated by a describable movement that's so strong nothing can or could stop it. Whatever *takes place* happens on this site, and can't be justified or dismissed on principle. It's not a position but a movement, containing every possible process. My thought is anthropomorphism ripped to pieces. I don't want to reduce or assimilate everything that exists to a paralyzed slavery but to the wild *impossibility* that I am, an impossibility that can't avoid limits but can't stay inside them either. At this moment *Unwissenheit*—desirable non-

* The impossibility of knowing the future.

knowledge—becomes an expression of hopeless wisdom. Reaching the limit of its development and longing to be "put to death," thought rushes precipitously to the arena of sacrifice. And just as an emotion grows similarly until sobs burst it apart, thought's fullness takes it to the point of being blown down by the wind, and contradiction rages at last.

With any tangible reality, for each being, you have to find the place of sacrifice, the wound. A being can only be touched where it yields. For a woman, this is under her dress; and for a god it's on the throat of the animal being sacrificed.

Once you've come to hate the egotism of being alone, once you've ecstatically tried to lose yourself, you've had your hands around the empty reaches of heaven's throat: heaven has to howl, has to let its blood flow. Undressed, a woman's open to you, she's a field of delight (modestly clothed, did she trouble you?). There's a similarity here: how, when heaven's empty reaches are torn apart, they open to you, and how, when the body's nakedness gives itself to you, you're lost.

History is incomplete. When this book is read, the outcome of the war taking place now will be known to the smallest schoolchild. I am writing at a time when nothing can give me the knowledge that schoolchild has. Wartime reveals the incompleteness of history, so much so that it's shocking to die a few days before the end (it's like reading an adventure story and putting down the book ten pages before the conclusion). To be in tune with history's incompleteness (something death implies) is a privilege vouchsafed only occasionally to the living! Who but Nietzsche could have written, *Ich liebe die Unwissenheit um die Zukunft*?!* Against this…blind Resistance fighters dying sure of whatever outcome they wanted.

Knowledge, like history, is incomplete. I'll die with no answer to basic problems, forever ignorant of developments that will alter human perspectives (they'd change mine, just as they'll change those of future generations).

Each of us is incomplete compared to someone else—an animal's incomplete compared to a person…and a person compared to God, who is complete only to be imaginary.

* I love not knowing the future.

A man knows he's incomplete, then begins to suppose existence is complete and true. At this point he disposes not just of completion but (as a result) of incompletion. Until then the incomplete stemmed from his impotency, but with completeness available, a man's excess potency releases a desire for incompleteness in him. If he chooses, he can become humble, poor and—in God—enjoy his humility and poverty. He pictures God himself succumbing to the desire for incompletion, the desire to be human and poor, and to die in torment.

Theology's principle that "the world is complete" is maintained at every time and in all places, including the night of Golgotha. There's a necessity for God to be killed: to see the world in the weakness of incompletion. The next thought to occur is that, come what may, the world has to be *completed*, although this is what's impossible and incomplete. Everything real fractures and cracks. The illusion of an unmoving river is dissipated and the stagnant water starts to flow, and I hear the sound of the next waterfall.

The illusion of completeness which I'm (humanly) aware of in the body of a woman with her clothes on: as soon as she's even partly undressed, her animal nature becomes visible and (while I'm watching) hands me over to my own incompleteness.... The more perfect, the more isolated or confined to ourselves we are. But the wound of incompleteness opens me up. Through what could be called incompleteness or animal nakedness or the wound, the different separate beings *communicate*, acquiring life by losing it in *communication* with each other.

Some time ago when drunk and waiting for a subway on the platform at the Strasbourg/St. Denis stop, I used the back of a photo of a naked woman to write on. Along with something nonsensical I wrote, "Not to communicate signifies exactly the bloody necessity of communicating." I was rambling, but I hadn't lost consciousness and in silence endured an unbearable need to scream and be naked. At each stage, the same suffering. The need for ruin makes all life anguish; but because of this need, being escapes completion. The non-satisfaction implicit in the turmoil of history, the movement of knowledge that destroys every possibility of rest, the image of God that ends up only as torment, the desperately sick whore who lifts up her dress—so many means of "communication experienced as nakedness," without which everything is empty.

4 The Point of Ecstasy

More than a month ago I started this book as the result of an upheaval that ended up challenging everything and freed me from undertakings I was stuck in. Once war broke out, there was no way I could wait any more—wait, that is, for the liberation which this book is for me.

Chaos is the condition of this book and it's boundless in every sense. *I love* the idea that my moods and licentiousness are pointless. Underneath is a strong sense of purpose, unconcerned with my impatience, distant and indifferent to the dangers that entice it. I need, beyond anxiousness and beyond any measurable ambition, to completely accept my obvious destiny. It's as obvious and undefinable as being in love. I'd like to die of this fate.

I wanted ecstasy and found it. I call my fate the *desert* and I am not afraid of imposing this arid mystery. I want others to be able to be where I am, in this desert I assume they *miss*.

As directly as possible I'll talk about the paths I took to get to this ecstasy in the hope others will reach it the same way.

Life is a result of disequilibrium and instability. Stable forms are needed to make it possible however. Going from one extreme to the other, from one desire to another, from a state of collapse to frantic tension if the movement speeds up, there can only be ruin and emptiness. We have to stake out courses that are stable enough. To shrink from fundamental stability isn't less cowardly than to hesitate about shattering it. Perpetual instability is more boring than adhering strictly to a rule, and only what's in existence can be made to come into disequilibrium, that is, to be *sacrificed*. The more equilibrium the object has, the more *complete* it is, and the greater the disequilibrium or *sacrifice* that can result. These principles conflict with morality, which necessarily is a leveling force and an enemy to alternation. They destroy the romantic morality of confusion as much as they do the opposite morality.

The desire for ecstasy can't exclude method. I don't see why people object to this.

Method means doing violence to habits of relaxation.

Method isn't communicated in writing. Writing shows you the road taken. Other roads are still possible. The only truth, in general, is the inevitable ascent and tension.

There's nothing humiliating in either strictness or artifice. Method means swimming against a current. Your humiliation comes from the current; the means of going against it would seem pleasant even if they were worse.

The ebb and flow of meditation is like plant movements when a flower forms. Ecstasy isn't explanation, isn't justification, isn't clarification. What it is is a flower—as unfinished, as perishable. The only way out: take a flower, look at it till there's harmony in it, so that it explains, clarifies and justifies *because of* being unfinished, *because of* being perishable.

The way goes through a deserted region, which is, however, haunted (with ghosts of delight and fear). Beyond: are a blind man's motions, eyes wide open, arms stretching out, staring at the sun, and inside he's turning to light. Imagine now that a change takes place. There's a bursting into flame that's so sudden the idea of substance seems empty; place, exteriority, and image become so many empty words, and the words that have least shifted—*fusion* and *light*—are by nature incomprehensible. It's difficult talking about *love* (a discredited and ineffectual word) because of the fact that *subjects* and *objects* usually drag it down into impotence.

Can there be any speaking of a soul or of God? Or of love uniting these two terms? Or of a love like lightning that would be expressed by means of two terms that have apparently been least dragged down? That, to be frank, would be to drag them down most deeply of all.

An electrified train pulls into the Gare St-Lazare, and I'm inside leaning against a window. I want to stand clear of the weakness that sees this only as insignificant, given the immensity of the universe. If the world is given the value of being a completed totality, this is possible. But if there's only a partial universe or incompleteness, each part has no less meaning than the whole. I'd be ashamed to look for an ecstatic truth that raised me to the level of a completed universe but withdrew meaning from "the train pulling into the station."

Ecstasy is *communication* between terms (these terms aren't necessarily defined), and communication possesses a value the terms didn't have: it annihilates them. Similarly, the light of a star (slowly) annihilates the star itself.

Incompletion, the wound, and the pain that has to be there if communication is to take place. Completion—the contrary of this.

What's requisite for communication is a defect or "fault." Communication enters like death through a chink in the armor. What's required is an overlapping of two lacerations, mine, yours.

What seems "faultless" and stable—a whole that has a look of completion (house, person, street, landscape or sky). The "fault" or defect can appear though.

To be considered a whole, the whole needs mind, it can exist only in the mind. Similarly a lack of the whole can appear only in someone's mind. There's a subjective basis for "wholeness" and "lack of wholeness," though "lack of wholeness" is *profoundly* real. Since the whole is constructed arbitrarily, the perception of a defect amounts to seeing the construction as arbitrary. The "lack of wholeness" is *profoundly* real since it's perceived by means of imperfection in what is arbitrary. Imperfection is situated (like construction) in unreality…it leads to reality.
There are:
fragments that shift and change (objective reality);
a completed totality (appearance and subjectivity);
and a lack of totality (change when it's situated at the level of ap-

pearance but reveals reality as fragmented, changing, and incomprehensible).

Attracted to each other, a man and a woman connect through lust. The communication joining them depends on the nakedness of their laceration. Their love signifies that neither can see the being of the other but only a wound and a need to be ruined. No greater desire exists than a wounded person's need for another wound.

Alone, wounded, dedicated to his own ruin, a man faces the universe. If he sees the universe as a completed whole, he's in the presence of God. God—to follow human custom here—is everything that might happen, taken as a whole. The act of breaking up this apparent whole itself takes place at the level of appearance. The crucifixion, for example, is a wound by which believers communicate with God.

Nietzsche represented the "death of God" as later provoking a return to "a changing, fragmented, and incomprehensible reality."

On the same level you find—
> the ridiculous universe,
> a naked woman,
> and torment.

Imagining myself being tormented, I'm in ecstasies.
Nakedness gives me the painful need for amorous embraces.
But the universe leaves me unconcerned, it doesn't make me laugh—this is another empty notion.

Now this much is true: ecstasy's object isn't the universe. But it isn't a woman or torment either. Woman, in a human sense, is an invitation to ruin. Torment is frightening. But ecstasy's object can't be anything completely frightening or too human.
I'm back to "the ridiculous universe." If it's ridiculous it has to be different from a universe the idea of which doesn't make me laugh. Nonetheless, the universe that's ridiculous has to be a transposition; thinking of some sort of ridiculous element I've transposed it, keeping its perceptible aspects in my mind, while with my thought I deny its concreteness.

Even at the start I never considered anything concrete. I thought vaguely of something provoking laughter. And at this point I'm going

to bring in a joke—the last I heard. A man standing on a bench is painting an electric lightbulb blue but is having problems reaching it with
his brush. Another person comes in, goes over to him and tells him with
a poker-face, "Hold onto the brush, I'm going to pull this bench out."
I could have left this story out, but in this specific case "the change takes
place at the level of appearances." The mind viewed a coherent whole
—lightbulb, paintbrush, and painter being its parts. This whole has its
reality in your mind alone, so that a movement of mind is enough to
make it incomplete. But this doesn't produce a void. Just for an instant
the curtain of appearances gets ripped in two and in the rent the mind
glimpses "the ridiculous universe."

"Change at the level of appearance" was necessary for there to be a
return to "changing, fragmented, and incomprehensible reality."

There is some kind of identity among "woman," "torment," and "the
ridiculous universe"—my need for self-destruction comes from them.
But that's still a limited consideration. In the end what counts is the fact
of altering the habitual order—the impossibility of being unconcerned....

Later I'll get back to this line of thought, which sleep broke into (it
leads you to difficulties that are tedious...).

I've just looked at two photos of torture. I'd gotten used to the pictures, though one was so awful my heart skipped a beat.

I must have stopped writing. As I do sometimes, I went to sit by the
open window. No sooner was I seated than I fell into some kind of
trance. Unlike the other night when I doubted it painfully, this time the
fact this kind of state is more intense than erotic pleasure was clear to
me. I don't see *anything*—which is not a thing to be touched or seen.
That makes you sad and heavy from not dying. If in my anguish I picture everything I've loved, I should assume that the fugitive realities that
love connects me to are, so to speak, only so many clouds concealing
what is there. Ecstatic images can betray you. Only fright can totally
measure *what is there*. Fright made it happen: there had to be some
wrenching commotion for *it to be there*.

Again this time suddenly recalling *what is there*, I must have started
crying. I lift my empty head—empty because of love's strength and because of my state of being *in rapture*. I'm going to tell you how I arrived
at an ecstasy of such intensity. On the wall of appearance I threw images
of explosion and of being lacerated—ripped to pieces. First I had to
summon up the greatest possible silence, and I got so as to be able to

do this pretty much at will. In this boring silence, I evoked every possible way there was of my being ripped to pieces. Obscene, ridiculous, and deadly thoughts came rushing out one after the other. I thought of a volcano's depths, war, and my own death. It wasn't possible any more to doubt that ecstasy dispenses with any idea of God. I felt a feeling of mischievous distaste for the clerical and nun-like idea that a person must "give up the particular for the general."

On the first day the wall yielded I was in a forest at night. During part of the day I had experienced fierce sex feelings but hadn't allowed myself any satisfaction. I decided to take my desire to the limit by "meditating" (without revulsion) on images associated with it.

One long dark day succeeded another. When feelings of wild complicity peter out, the pleasures remain unbearable—crowds, on an empty stomach, milling around. What I should have done was express life's exuberance by shouting at the top of my lungs, but I couldn't do this. Too much jubilation turned into empty excitement. What I should have been: a whole throng of voices lifting loudly to heaven. The emotions that develop from "tragic night to light's dazzling glory" leave you sitting in your bedroom, dazed. Only a people could deal with these feelings....

But what a people can deal with, can infuse with intensity even, tortures me. Knowing what I want seems an impossibility now...there's excitement pricking at me like buzzing flies. It's just about that vague, but subjectively it reduces me to ashes. Shock, isolation, and continual moodiness in times of exhaustion produce mental disorder, at times reaching the edge of impossibility.

I think of this kind of confusion as inevitable. This thirst without thirst, tears like tears of a newborn child in its cradle, not knowing what it wants or what the purpose of its tears is, these act as *ultima verba*: they're the last broadcast to our world from dead suns that feed on the living one.

To enter the kingdom of tiny thirsts and tiny tears, you have to have the nonsensicality of an infant. Otherwise words break down in the void. You can't get there if you're still speaking, if the normal world where words keep their meanings still satisfies you. Only if, thanks to a lie, you think a *last word* can be added to what is said, only then would boasting be possible. You wouldn't see that the *last word* is no longer a word and that if you disrupt everything, there's nothing left to *say*. Screaming babies aren't capable of creating language since they don't experience that *need*.

What I know and can say:
Thirst without thirst needs too much to drink—tears a surfeit of exuberance. And the surfeit of drink needs thirst without any thirst; while a surfeit of exuberance wants, in its impotence, to be unable to cry in its experience of tears. If surfeit alone is the origin of my thirst and my tears, at least my surfeit wants this thirst and these tears. If other people, complaining of thirst and in tears or dry-eyed, want *speech* in addition, I have less respect for them than for children. (Children aren't aware of what they're doing when they cheat.) If I cry out or weep myself, I come to realize my joy is freed in this way. And so: the sound of thunder is still the sound of thunder if, as I perceive it, it's only distant rumbling. My memory isn't failing and I become almost a baby, instead of a philosopher nursing his melancholy or a poet living on the margins (as if having only half my memory or a quarter of it). And more: the idea that misery like this, a (mute) suffering like this, might be a last *breath* of what we are, remains in me like a secret, a secret collusion with the ungraspable, unintelligible nature of things. Pleasurable squealing, baby-like laughter, premature exhaustion, I'm made of all this and it delivers me naked and cold to the blows of fate. But from the bottom of my heart *I want* to be naked.

As what is unreachable opens up to me, I let go of first uncertainties—fear of banal blissful content. Contemplation of the object of ecstasy becomes less an effort and I can say of it that it lacerates me, cuts me. And like a razor's edge cutting, it's a point crying out, it blinds me. It's not a point since it fills me. Provocative, bitter nakedness is an arrow and sails out towards it.

What's "communicated" (from this site to a person and from a person to this site) is lightning-like loss.
The need to go astray, to be destroyed is an extremely private, distant, passionate, turbulent truth, and has nothing to do with what we call substance.
Particulars are required if there is to be loss and merger. Without particulars (somewhere on the planet a train is pulling into a station or something just as empty) nothing could be "set free." The difference between sacrifice (sacredness) and (theological) divine substance can be easily noted. *Sacredness* is the opposite of substance. Christianity's

mortal sin is associating sacredness with "generality creating particularity." Nothing is sacred if it hasn't first been individual (although afterwards it's no longer that).

Ecstasy is different from receiving sex pleasure, but less different from giving it.

I don't give anything. I'm illuminated by an (impersonal) outer joy that seems sure and I *intuit* it. I'm consumed by this awareness as I'm consumed by a woman when making passionate love. The "point" that "cries out" is similar to an orgasm in human beings, and the idea we have of it is like the idea of a "pleasure point"—or orgasm—in the throes of sex.

I wanted to speak as clearly as possible about the "means of ecstasy." I haven't succeeded very well, but I've tried.

Method in meditation is analogous to technique in sacrifice. The point of ecstasy is bared if inside myself I shatter individuality that confines me to myself. So too sacredness replaces an animal in the exact moment the priest kills or destroys it.

Chancing on an image of torture, I can turn away in fright. But if I look I'm *beside myself*.... The confining and limiting world of my individual being opens when, horrified, I see torture. A sight of torture opens my individual being violently, lacerates it.

What doesn't follow is that through laceration I can reach a beyond which in vague terms I'll call THE ESSENCE OF WORLDS.

Unacceptable terms and too vague…but I'll stick with them. Only by using *negative* distinctions can the vagueness be reduced.
First:
THE ESSENCE OF WORLDS isn't God. A glimpse of THE ESSENCE OF WORLDS once and for all cancels the possibility of immutable stagnation threatened by that ridiculous syllable…;
in the second place:
THE ESSENCE OF WORLDS isn't in any way opposed to the vertiginous, catastrophic movement sweeping, into an abyss, both us and everything that comes from some immense terrifying depth and emerges as solid or apparently solid.
(To be honest, the vision of an "essence of worlds" is one of generalized catastrophe, a catastrophe that can't be stopped by anything....

The vision of THE DEATH OF GOD doesn't differ at all, but shakes us from a theological sleep and finally is alone in its capacity to answer the most reasonable demands.)

It's so true to say that death takes people's measure that far from succumbing to fright, it's actually a vision of fright that delivers us.

Instead of avoiding laceration I'd deepen it. The sight of torture staggered me, but quickly enough…I greeted the sight with lack of concern. I'm calling to mind the innumerable torments of a throng as it dies. Finally (or rather all at once) human immensity gets consigned to unlimited horror….
Cruelly I stretch the laceration out—in that instant attaining ecstasy. *Compassion*, pain, and ecstasy connive with each other.

A man sometimes will want to be free of useful objects—free of work and the slavishness useful objects entail. In the same development useful objects have been responsible for our circumscribed individuality (short-sighted egotism) and the general banality of all our life. Work founded humanity, but at the summit humanity is freed from work.

The time is coming to free human life from limited activity and bring the weighty abandonment of sleep into opposition with the necessity for mechanical motion. The time is coming to halt the flight of speech inside the mind and, in that emptiness, steep it with the kind of calm that results in images and words which when they occur appear strange and unattractive.

Simple *concentration* is deceptive and irritating. It's contrary to life's natural movement towards the outside (usually, it's true, this movement is abortive and leads to useful objects). The pleasurable sluggishness into which the mind enters is all the more exhausting because it depends on artifice….

I advise maintaining a relaxed but also steady and alert body posture. Personal opportunities exist, but we can first trust proven expedients: deep breathing and concentration of attention on breath as an intuited secret of all life. As equivalent to the flow of images and to cope with the flight of ideas from the fact of endless association, we can suggest an unchanging riverbed with the help of repeated phrases or words. Is this procedure unwarranted? Often enough it's dismissed by those who put up with much more and are at the beck and call of mechanisms these techniques can halt.

If interfering is *obnoxious* (sometimes inevitably you love what you'd rather detest), the most serious aspect isn't submitting to constraints but the danger of excessive appeal. The first operation sets you free and bewitches you. But being free finally is disgusting: it's boring and unmanly to live in a state of bewitchment.

For a period of several days, life enters empty dark. A wonderful feeling of relaxation is the result, and unlimited power is disclosed to the mind. The world is at your feet and you can do what you want. Only problems soon develop.

In the first stage, the traditional teachings are irrefutable—they're wonderful. I got them from a friend, who got them from an Asian source. I'm not unaware of Christian practices, which are more authentically dramatic; they lack a first movement, without which we remain subordinated to speech.

A few Christians have broken from the language world and come to the ecstatic one. In their case, an aptitude has to be supposed which made mystical experience inevitable *in spite of Christianity's essential reliance on speech*.

5 Thick as Thieves

...occasional luck—my luck—in a world that seems increasingly terrible makes me tremble.

The circumstances of my life are paralyzing.
Possibly?
I'm solidly convinced one day I'm going to see in its clarity "everything that is"—quick or dead. Sunset . . . night's almost upon us. Streaked with clouds, the star-studded sky, the hill: beyond (possibly?) stretch spaces that are only dreams or a need for space. It hardly matters whether or not I see them: the laughter and tears suffice, being impossible like the world is. In this playful mood the whole world becomes a game being played—and its supporting unreality is able to step outside itself and see itself there. When it does this another time it'll see itself another way.

A return to animal life, lying on the bed, a pitcher of red wine with two glasses. I don't think I've ever seen the sun go down so flamboyantly in a sky which is scarlet and gold with pink clouds that go on and on, forever. Slowly, innocence, whimsicality, and a kind of decayed magnificence work me to a fever pitch.

Luck gets you high like wine does. But words fail. Spent by the rush and *intuiting*, drained by it.

The Chinese executioner of my photo haunts me: there he is busily cutting off his victim's leg at the knee. The victim is bound to a stake, eyes turned up, head thrown back, and through a grimacing mouth you see teeth.

The blade's entering the flesh at the knee. Who can accept that a horror of this magnitude would express "what you are" and lay bare your nature?

An anecdote about an intense experience from a few months ago. I went to a forest at nightfall. I walked for an hour, then hid along a dark path, where I wanted to find relief from an obsessive sexual feeling that weighed me down. Then at a point, it occurred to me how essential it was to break through complacency. I evoked the image of a bird of prey going for the throat of a smaller bird. I thought of dark leafy branches turning on me, turning on my complacency, aroused with the anger of a predatory bird. The impression I got was of a dark bird swooping down on me...and opening my throat.

This illusion of the senses wasn't as successful as others I've had. I shrugged it off and I think I started to laugh at that point—saved from going overboard on horror and uncertainty. In the depth of the dark everything was clear. On the way home, in spite of being exhausted, I walked on coarse pebbles (which normally would have twisted my feet) light and airy as a shadow. At that instant I wasn't expecting a thing, but the heavens opened and I *saw*. I *saw*: what a person can be kept from seeing only through intentional heaviness. All the useless fuss of the stifling day at last cracked open like an eggshell and was volatilized in the air.

As I walked on, the black sky in front of me grew lurid. Off in the distance a storm flashed lightning with no let-up—flickering, soundless, huge. Suddenly high dark silhouettes of trees were outlined in a brief flood of light. But this exuberance of sky paled when compared to the dawn that now appeared. Not precisely in me. I can't localize something that's as impossible to grasp—as sudden—as the wind.

Dawn came up all around me and I was sure of it. With the little consciousness left in me, I was lost in the dawn. Violence is soft and the sharpest razor nicked compared to this dawn! Bliss to no purpose, useless, a naked hand grips the blade—and blood spurts out in ecstasy.

With whatever passion and cruel lucidity I can bring to bear, inside of me I wanted life *to be naked*. I've been working on this book since the war broke out and everything else is emptiness as far as I'm concerned. Now all I want is to live—intoxication, ecstasy, my existence as naked as a woman's when wracked with desire.

As the life I am is revealed to me and at the same time, because I've lived it without hiding anything, as it becomes visible on the outside: inside me what's left is blood, tears, and lust.

This happy laughter, my nights of joy, all my aggressive wantonness, this wind-slashed cloud is (as it may be) only a long sob. It leaves me chilled, thrown back on the desire for impossible nakedness.

What I eagerly embrace. Or again, what I don't embrace—the impossible and marvellous. Everything is emptied out and resolved in a hiccup.

Naked whores (partly stripped naked) like a hiccup or like a creaking floor.

There's something chilling about sulfur fumes. At the top of stockings, a belly—those conniving eyes leave you with little hope of love! What untamed, gentle cruelty there is in nakedness.

A woman's nakedness yearns for a man's nakedness as eagerly as inflamed pleasure yearns for anguish.

A pipe, two white detachable collars, one blue, four black hats that belong to women: four hats with different shapes to put on tombstones in the shape of a cross.

People's nakedness is as provoking as their graves, and the bad smells make me laugh. The grave is as *inevitable* to a person as being *stripped bare*.

A request you ought to make to your boyfriend or girlfriend: be the victim of the impossible.

(I didn't write that last calmly, I'd been drinking.)

I can't abide sentences…. Everything I've asserted, convictions I've expressed, it's all ridiculous and dead. I'm only silence, and the universe is silence.

The world of words is laughable. Threats, violence, and the blandishments of power are part of *silence*. Deep complicity can't be expressed in words.

Acting like a master means never being held accountable. The idea of *explaining* what I do makes me sick!

Sovereignty isn't speaking—or it's deposed.

Future holiness will long for evil.

Speak of justice and you *are* justice. You are suggesting a system of justice. A father or a guide.

I'm not recommending justice.

The friendship I have to contribute belongs to an accomplice.

Feeling wildly exuberant, a sense of license, of immature—and hellish—pleasure!

Only "sovereign" being knows ecstasy, if ecstasy isn't accorded by God!

The revelation that applies to my experience is that of a man seeing himself. It assumes lust and spite which morality can't inhibit—and a contented friendship with spiteful and lewd people. Man is his own law as he confronts the sight of his own nakedness.

Confronting God, the mystic took on the attitude of a *subject*. If you confront existence, you have the attitude of a *sovereign*.

Holiness encourages existence's complicity with lust, cruelty, and spite.

To the lustful, the cruel, and the spiteful, the *holy man* brings friendship, laughter thick as thieves—or complicity.

The *saint's* friendship quietly assumes that it will be betrayed. This is the sort of friendship you have with *yourself*, when you know you'll die. When you realize maybe death will *intoxicate* you . . .

6 Incomplete

Thought reflects the universe, and thought is the most changing thing —it isn't any less the reality of the universe. And since there's no small or large in it, and since the tiniest part has no less meaning than the whole (no more meaning and no less), "what is" differs as a function of time. Imagining an ingathering at the end of time (Hegel) or outside time (Plato) is surely a mental necessity. This necessity is real: it's the condition of meaning, above and without which thought can't conceive of anything—yet it's subject to change. But why limit these perspectives to some subjective reality opposing an unchanging, objective one? One possibility is given by looking at the world as a fusion of subject and object, a possibility in which subject, object, and fusion wouldn't stop changing, so there would be several types of identity. This wouldn't mean thought necessarily attains the real but *possibly* attains it. It would mean only fragments come into play: reality wouldn't be unified, but composed of successive or coexistent fragments (fragments with changing limits).

Constant human errors would express the incomplete character of reality—and so of truth. Knowledge proportionate to its object—if that object is incomplete in its very being—would develop in every way. This knowledge would be, as totality, a huge architecture in deconstruction and construction, both at the same time, uncoordinated or barely so, but never through and through so they overlap. Looking at things this way, being human isn't so bad. Otherwise, isn't it idiotic picturing the degradation out of which our dull minds and foolishness would issue? Unless God—completed being—wasted away with desire for incompleteness, for tininess, you could say, which would be greater than his absence of true greatness. (There wouldn't be greatness in God: there's no difference or comparison in him.)

This amounts to seeing humanness and its errors as a mirror that isn't perfect and isn't deforming, nature being only a fragment reflected in the mirror we are.

This proposition isn't grounded (there aren't answers to decisive questions). We can only attribute the questions—the fact that there's no answer to them—to the portion of reality that is our lot. But what if I admit there's no general rule capable of subordinating parts (making them dependent on something greater than they are)? Questions (and answers that aren't forthcoming) are limits, to be found in some way in different possibilities.

These propositions and presuppositions aren't grounded, nor could they be: nothing is grounded but on some necessity that excludes other possibilities. They constitute only remnants of a wholeness belonging to someone who speaks long after the construction of the foundations, when their destruction is complete.

It's difficult to think otherwise: "two and two are four" is a truth that applies to every reality, every possibility! If this is insisted on…there's nothing else to be discovered in the empty reaches of the universe other than this obvious formula (which is as empty as the universe).

If someone wants to use this unique, empty certainty as a pedestal and make it the basis of a stubborn dignity—can I laugh any less than at the other idea, that "two and two are five"? When in a disruptive mood I tell myself, "two and two are five…so why not?" I'm really not giving it any thought, and everything at that moment is escaping me. But *as every object escapes me inside myself* I am certainly not approaching less closely to whatever it is that comes under the rubric of knowledge than if, understanding "two and two are four" as an eternal truth, I believed I could attain the secret of things.

As I write, a ladybug flies under my lamp and alights on my hand; I lift her off and put her on a sheet of paper. A while ago I copied out one of Hegel's schemas on the paper, a diagram showing the various forms he has for getting from one extremity to the other, from *Allgemeinheit* to *Einzelheit*.* She stopped in the *Geist* column, where you go from *allegemeiner Geist* to *sinnliches Bewusstsein* (*Einzelheit*)† by way of *Volk*, *Staat*, and *Weltgeschichte*.‡ Moving along on her perplexed way she drops into a column marked *Leben*** (her home territory) before getting to the center column's "unhappy consciousness," which is only nominally relevant to her.

I'm humiliated by this pretty little bug. I lack any happy consciousness in her presence, and it takes me a great deal of effort to distance myself from the unhappiness of other people. Pushy people take advantage of this unhappiness, and when I fall prey to it, that is what I become myself.

Your unhappy philosopher needs a drink, just like your working man needs soap. You get dirty by working, just like you get sober by doing philosophy.

Do I have a conclusion? If I treat my thinking to a drink, a brighter day dawns for my consciousness!

The tenor of my thinking isn't as much philosophical unhappiness as it is auspicious dislike for the (obvious) bankruptcy of thinking. If I need a drink, it's so a little of other people's dirt will rub off on me.

Should a person be humble reading Lautréamont or Rimbaud? That would be just another kind of unhappy consciousness! You can get just as pushy with this one as with the other.

Read two "talks" by a Hindu monk I know and had seen for an hour or so—his elegance, his handsomeness in his pink robe, and the friendly energy of his laughter pleased me. Depressed with writing that sticks to Western standards.

Here's something to express forcefully, to keep clearly in mind—that there's no truth when people look at each other as if they're separate individuals. Truth starts with conversations, shared laughter, friendship

* From universality to individuality.
† From universal mind to sensory consciousness (individuality).
‡ People, State, and World History.
** Life.

and sex, and it only happens *going from one person to another*. I hate the thought of a person being connected to isolation. The recluse who has the impression he reflects the world is ridiculous to my mind. He can't reflect it because, being himself a center of the reflection, he stops being able to relate to *what doesn't have a center*. As I picture it, the world doesn't resemble a separate or circumscribed being but *what goes from one person to another* when we laugh or make love. When I think this is the way things are, immensity opens and I'm lost.

How little *self* matters then! And *reciprocally*, can the presence of an unfamiliar person be of any concern to me?

I don't believe in God—from inability to believe in self.

Belief in God is belief in self. God is only a guarantee given to me. If we didn't project the *self* on the absolute we'd be convulsed with laughter.

If I give my life to life itself to be lived and ruined (I don't want to say, to mystical experience), I open my eyes on a world in which I have no meaning unless I'm wounded, torn apart and *sacrificed*, and in which divinity, in the same way, is just a tearing apart or being torn apart, is executing or being executed, is sacrifice.

If you practice meditation, God, they say, is as necessary as one terminal to another in generating an electric spark. For the ecstatic outpouring to take place, there has to be an object proposed: even if reduced to a point, this object possesses such power to destroy that it's natural, even easy to give it a name. But the danger, they also say, can't be denied—that the terminal (the ponderousness) to which the name God is assigned would take precedence over the ecstatic outflashing. In truth, the object or point in front of me and towards which my ecstasy is aimed is precisely what others have seen and described when speaking of God. We're reassured when something is stated clearly, and defining an immutable SELF as the principle of our being and nature presents the temptation to make the object of meditation something clear. Such a definition projects what we are into infinity or eternity. The idea of an individual existence is conducive to setting up an object towards which ecstasy can be directed (setting up an object can conceivably aid its discovery in ecstasy). To set up an object isn't any less an obnoxious limit, because in the spark of ecstasy the necessary subject/object terminals are necessarily consumed—they have to be annihilated. This means that as the subject is destroyed in meditation, the object (god or God) also is a dying victim. (Otherwise the situation of ordinary life, the subject locating some useful object, would preserve the servility inherent in action, whose standard is utility.)

I didn't choose God as an object, but humanly, the young Chinese (a condemned felon) shown in the photos as covered with blood while the executioner tortures him (the blade's already in his knee-bone). I was connected to this unhappy being in ties of horror and friendship. But when I looked at this image to the *point of harmony*, the necessity of being only myself was cancelled. And at the same time this object I chose disintegrated into vastness and, in a storm of pain, was destroyed.

Each person is a stranger to the universe, belonging as he or she does to objects, meals, newspapers, which by circumscribing us and creating our *individuality* leave us ignorant of all else. What connects existence to *all else* is death; looking at death, you stop belonging to your room, to family and friends—you're part of heaven's free play.

To better grasp this, think of an opposition from physics: wave versus particle. The first accounts for phenomena by assuming there are waves (light, vibrations of the air or ocean waves). The second sees the world composed of corpuscles (neutrons, photons, or electrons) whose minimal combinations are atoms or molecules. Is the leap from lovemaking to light waves, or from personal existence to corpuscles, a forced or arbitrary one? Perhaps. But still, problems of physics clarify the way two images of life are opposed: one erotic and religious, the other profane and matter-of-fact. One is open, the other closed. Making love is such an entire negation of isolated existence that we find it natural, even wonderful in a sense, that an insect dies in the consummation it sought out. And this excess has its counterpart in the urge of one person to possess another. This need doesn't just color the expression of erotic emotions; it also governs the reciprocal and proprietary relations that obtain between the worshipper and a darkly divine presence. (God becomes the property of the believer just as the believer in turn becomes God's.) This happens necessarily. But knowing it isn't the same as submitting to it. The "point" I've mentioned (a lacerating and lamenting point) so radiates life (although…no, since…it's the same as death) that once having been bared, the object of a dream or desire confused with it takes on a life of its own, even goes up in flames and is intensely present. From the moment of its "apparition," the divinity becomes available like a beloved or like a woman giving you her nakedness in the throes of love. A god torn by wounds and a woman at the edge of pleasure transcribe ecstasy's outcry. It's easy and even inevitable to transcribe it; we only have to fix our gaze on what's in front of us. But in attaining the object in my outcry, I know I've destroyed what deserves to be called "object." Just as nothing now keeps me from my death (which I love while finding a drowning pleasure that summons its coming), I still have to link the sign of my laceration and annihilation to discernible faces corresponding with my need to love.

Human destiny has met with pity, morality, and the most divergent attitudes (an asphyxiating anguish or horror more often than not), but it can scarcely be said we've encountered friendship. Not until Nietzsche....

Writing's always only a game played with ungraspable reality. And given the impossibility of enclosing the world with propositions, I wouldn't even want to try. I wanted rapturousness for the *living*—for non-believers who find happiness in the pleasures of the world—a rapturousness that seemed distant from them (and which, so far, ugly asceticism has jealously kept away from them). If people never had the urge to look for pleasure (or joy) and if the only thing that mattered was repose (satisfaction) and equilibrium, then the gift I'm contributing would be without meaning. This gift is ecstasy, it's a fitful play of lightning....

These days I sleep "fitfully," my dreams are heavy and violent—they match my intense weariness....

The day before yesterday I discovered I was on the slopes of an enormous volcano, like Etna, though more like a Sahara extending out into the distance. Its lava was dark-colored sand. I drew near the crater and if it wasn't day, it wasn't night either, but some unspecific time in between. Even before I made out the outline of the crater clearly enough, I knew it was an active volcano. High above the place where I was (I thought I was near the summit) an immense wall reared up—the color and consistency of sand, but smooth and vertical. An image of approaching catastrophe, its fiery flow of lava streamed slowly down the wall into darkness. I turned around and saw the deserted countryside striped with long plumes of smoke trailing low and hugging the ground. I headed down the mountainside knowing I couldn't escape, that I was doomed. I felt utter anguish: I wanted to gamble, but the game turned against me. Through the smoke plumes I soon gained the foot of the mountain—but where I hoped for a way out, I saw only slopes rising in all directions. I was at the bottom of an irregular funnel—long white trails of stifling volcanic fumes drifted out of the cracked walls. I was overtaken by the certainty of death but I went on, and the path became more and more difficult. I came to the entrance of a cave. Inside were rocks laid out in geometric configurations, entrancingly brilliant with their raw yellows, blues, and blacks, the colors of butterfly wings. As I made my way deeper towards safety I entered a huge hall, the architecture of which was no less beautiful and geometrical than the entrance. Several figures there stood out with much less distinctness than statues on a cathedral porch. They were of such scale and serenity as to strike me with fear. I'd never seen or imagined beings this perfect, this powerful, this lucidly ironic. One of them rose before me in his majestic and glacial architecture, though seated in a casual position, as if the rows of figures along the frieze of which he was a part were waves of clear, purified laughter with no more hindrance and no less violence than breakers in a storm. Standing in front of this stone being, from whom there streamed an inner intoxicating lunar light, in a fit of desperation and in the certainty of sharing the mirth that stirred in him, I discovered (as I trembled) the power *to realize what I was*—and laugh. I faced him and, in spite of my confusion, expressed what I felt with deceptive ease: that I was like him and like those others akin to him, beings I saw still further back in the dark recesses engaged in laughter —a calm, frigid, lacerating laughter directed at my utter fear and unthinkable boldness. At this point my tension became such that I awoke.

A day or two earlier I dreamed the time had almost come when I'd stop being able to count on anything, when I'd let myself go without hindrance. What I desired so possessed me, I was swept, raised up on waves of wild eloquence. As in the more obscure volcano dream it was always death (desired and feared at the same time—and essentially consisting of the empty grandeur and unbearable laughter dreams allow), it was always death suggesting the leap, the power to connect up with a totally unknown blackness, which in fact won't ever be really known and whose appeal, not in the least inferior to even the most iridescent colors, consists in what it won't ever have, not the smallest speck of knowledge, since it's the annihilation of the system that had the power of knowing.

September 1939/March 1940

MISFORTUNES OF THE PRESENT TIME

1 Orphans of the Storm: Exodus

I'm starting a second notebook during the battle for the North. I can't say exactly why…I feel there's a dark necessity on me. I'm driven, scattered, tangled, I feel there's a curse.

During the night between May 9th and 10th, I really had no idea at all, and I kept waking up (which isn't like me), moaning and groaning in my pillow, a wreck, begging for mercy!…

Came down that morning into a sunny garden flooded with light. I saw the old man—the one they call Major—on the other side of the gate with a blue gardener's smock on. In an obliging country voice, excited but without going into details, he tells me the news he just got from the radio—the Germans in Belgium and in Holland.

I only feel loathing for romanticism—I'm as hard-headed as they come. The chaos in me is from an inability to put my strength to good *use*. I tore up (or lost) the letter to Blank, where I said that with the end of history there'll be no more use for negativity.* Negativity—and I was relying on Hegel—means action that results in disruption. Negativity that's not put to use would destroy whoever lived it—*sacrifice* will illuminate the conclusion of history as it did its dawn.

Sacrifice can't be for us what it was at the beginning of "time." Our experience is one of impossible appeasement. Lucid holiness recognizes in itself the need to destroy, the necessity for a tragic outcome.

---

* I found the text later, and it appears at the start of the Appendix.

I'm going (for a few hours) to a town I'm taken back to by horrible memories of my early years (my family lived there)—memories I'll have to put aside like the damned do, through laughter. I see myself as drawing near a tragic decline, which sometimes paralyzes me and sometimes cheers me.... Why write this down? I'm coming to the day when I'll rediscover remote parts of my life that'll mix uneasily with what seems important to me today. (What's to keep me from kicking at the altar step where maybe I'll shed my blood?)

Veiled, arid, misty, dazzling, an awareness of feelings turned to ashes. The calm of cinders. Strength that's absolutely certain—a pall of silence. Nothing true any more, since my heart stops bleeding.

Great and terrible events are difficult to deal with. But it's also true I wouldn't have wanted to live without them, even if what they brought me minute by minute was worse.

Often timid, uncourageous: left breathless by too much imagination.

H. is dead, I'd gotten to quite like him, he'd show up like a ghost slipping in—an affable old spook. I didn't see him often. Events ate away at him, left him horror-stricken—a strange kind of victim!

I've many times crossed Place de la Concorde, where in the old days the Terror took place. All rights belong to the people. And if some don't, the people can offer these up to the necessity that impels them! The people even have the right to ignore the suffering they require. It's logical and *naked* that H. should be dead.

I'd be ridiculous saying, "I love the people"—since I'm the same as they are. Lacerated though *absent*. The laceration is disturbing enough, but the absence more so. I wouldn't be able to say "I love..." Speaking exasperates me most of all. Silence, only silence answers the condition of my laceration!

The train I'm writing this on goes through a place hit by bombs Monday—sores you wouldn't necessarily notice...they have their own agenda—first signs of plague.

There's a price to pay for not facing things! This very morning, which I should have foreseen, all hell broke loose.

What I see (more or less) light-heartedly: in everything I write there's the mark of death, of coming closer and closer to it (the only thing that gives my writing its coherence).

Will I be able to retain this (Nietzschean) light-heartedness? (I don't know.)

As a heading for the preceding I wanted to write these four words—*the moment of truth*—referring to the critical moment of the bullfight: when the wounded beast sees death approaching. Trickery? With death—how could anyone *not* resort to cheating? Trickery! I made up my mind to die the other day: what came in with my anguish went out with the next wind.

This afternoon. Myself and the "sententious old man" pacing up and down the garden. I'd already seen him Tuesday. Then I was struck by our almost complete agreement about things—at the exact moment when everything's teetering. As far as he was concerned, the dialectic of autonomy and communication couldn't have been clearer. What he wanted from my country couldn't be given by another country, wouldn't be touched by defeat.

The old man talking with me again for a long time June 5th, speaking, in a somewhat faltering logic, of our lives as saints' lives, lives we'd have in a world belonging to the enemy. As I write I'm about to leave Paris, and Paris at 8:00 in the morning is covered with a cloud of soot. I'm in a hotel in the middle of town and it's depressing. The end of the world is finally here—but what's to understand? I'm trying, on the fifth floor, to lose myself in meditation: to let myself be dissolved—through writing—in the hideous fog. Horror rises in my throat like vomit but I rely on my strength, it branches out and spreads like a tree. People want to keep suffering to the point of nausea. All the same they're possessed of strength.

Fatigue weighing so oppressively. A feeling of some unlimited disaster that personally (if barely) I'll escape, its impact revealed in stories you hear: dead children, screaming women, crowds out of control. Skyline of the city of Tours in flames, streaked with anti-aircraft fire. There's a shelter of some kind nearby, but I imagine not getting there. The worst is still to come, but slowly each difficulty is obviated (waiting cancelled out the desire). A little more effort! A little effort? I'm at the stage of laughing calmly at myself, I'm the butt of heaven's ill will. A peace and calm I think of as religious—a religious offering to darker deities.

While I write this, the "sententious old man" is dying. (He died two months later.)

Something in the infinitely complicated evasions and dodges of the human face parallels the *mind* at work—it's the basis of everything. What's gone is the capacity for reducing life to the simplicity of a sun. That simplicity is in us all, we abandon it for complications of chance, dependent on the greedy anguish of *self*.

Imagine a star being caught up in human foolishness. A polite "good morning!" to the sun would tell you quite a lot about the difference between the universe and humanness.

I wouldn't give up *laughing* for anything! Although we aren't "the sun" enough and I don't have it in me to burst into laughter at our smallness.
When the foundation of things totters, it's natural, keeping your eyes straight ahead, to wish for simplicity.

Without wings and alive! We had them once! We didn't fly.
Going from city to city in this rented car. Depressing and over-crowded cities—the chaos of defeat extending into the valleys. Low clouds, and the rain doesn't let up.

The car took the mountain route, through low-lying clouds that shrouded the base. You can't imagine a more dismal world. What we saw (now and then) was enough—the hostility, emptiness, and desolate condition of the region gave us a feeling of stunned immensity.
If the clouds had parted, the incomparably beautiful landscape would have fascinated us. Bright colors would have set off the dull nakedness. Glistening air (more or less sky) and shifting views would have revealed strangeness, sudden precipices, lushness. But only the anguish associated with the nakedness of these tablelands and a gloom induced by the empty space about them could have kept us in suspense as we looked at that spectacle.

I went from house to house—came into rooms filled with refugees, women and children pushing up against each other. From one of the most crowded there was a sound like a pig snorting. A little girl stretched out on a couch made this sound as she breathed in and out, a monster with rat-like legs, her inflamed face marked with disease.
According to A., Kierkegaard gives Job the right to shout his protests to heaven. I hate shouting. I *want* the conditions of the "land surveyor"—which as A. puts it are a game making the impossible pos-

sible. In that game at least—speech and language categories don't settle things.

Granted the emptiness of my village here (my strange and disconnected life), I'm not going to let it get to me.

What about kindness and accepting things? But what about, in that case, the "land surveyor"? And what about the fact that I can tell I'm laughing, guilty of being *a self*? Of not being someone else? Of not being dead? If you insist on it, I admit I'll have to pay the penalty. Only why not also laugh.

My light-heartedness is an arrow, released with enormous strength.

The misfortune goes on spreading. Of the world I was born into, the one that made me what I am, soon there'll be nothing left but a ruined memory.

Anguish—or dread—is the truth of Kierkegaard, and especially it's the truth of Kafka's "land surveyor." But is it mine? If I laugh and, laughing, perceive what's here and what's distant, what should I say to people who listen to me? Let them twist in their anguish!

Without choking in the low-lying fog, you'll possess the light like a fool—thinking it's your due. But can there be innocence in the world once the category "guilty" is introduced? Remembering the horrible things of the fog where your life ends, you know, on the contrary, that it's you who are due to the intoxicating day.

I've charted a path leading to the very spot where the river of individual beings is entirely lost in the ocean. Unceasingly, this river of intoxications and sufferings is lost in an ocean which is its glory—*glory that isn't a possession of any single individual.*

Looking at the naked mountain slopes in front of me while I "meditate," I imagine a horror emanating from them in cold and storms. Hostility of insects in combat—promise of death, not life!

The ridiculous truth of space opening up to me like marshy love-truths when you lift a skirt.

But eroticism requires an expenditure of too much strength…When you let go, nothing's left. Sade himself failed to understand that it's not some wicked stepmother, nature, that intends malevolence and obscenity, but *sanctity*—a human body's ecstasies. I write to take possession of that secret.... It would have escaped me if I hadn't undressed so many prostitutes. But I had to have the strength to go on. An explosion, lightning in the throat, is the gift offered to me.... What could be more desirable?

I add this. In the doorway of *glory* I found death, who appeared as nudity dressed in garters with long black stockings. The closer death got to being human the more terrible her fury. This Fury who put my hand in hers and took me straight to hell.

Cover my face with ashes? The mountain tule fogs spread their mourning...but it's not that I don't *already* know death. My eyes get lost in wallcrannies where dust and spiders show you ultimate truth: innocent cruelty on guard, ready to respond to the slightest inattentiveness. The cow's attention strays for a moment—her wound's covered with flies.

From September to June, to the extent that war was going on, my awareness of it consisted of anguish. I saw in the war something ordinary life lacked—something that causes fear and prompts horror and anguish. I turned to it to lose my thinking in horror—for me, war was torment, falling off a rooftop, a volcano erupting. I despise the boorishness of people drawn to the combat aspect of war; it attracted me by provoking anguish. War professionals, so called, are unfamiliar with these feelings. War is an activity that answers their needs. They go to the front to avoid anguish. Give it your all! That's what they think counts.

But what about those who rush away from the dangers of war like Christians shunning places of ill repute? And those who, in anguish, lack the courage to meet danger head on?!

Daylight floods the badlands, immersing them. Sound of insects from one end of the sky to the other. The pleasure is an Arabic one for me: invisible insects of the air, so many Aissaohs, a raucous chirring...space itself convulsed.

In the distance, eroded mountains, desolate and naked, rising from valley shadows. Inaccessible to human arrangement.

After a two-month collapse (going through Vichy).

What I despise most is the pettiness of the rich—who diminish whatever they look at. And morose whores! Seeing them, I'm speechless.

Could even death's weighty silence make them shut their mouths? The disaster goes too far, the pretense too glaring.

In anguish...no *end* of it in sight. Everything exhausts, too many obstacles exhausting me.

Others resist their anguish. They laugh, sing. They're *innocent*—and I'm *guilty*. What am I as far as they're concerned? Cynical, devious, a difficult person...an *intellectual*. How can I stand the weight of this dislike, this misunderstanding? I accept it. It's the excess of it that shocks me.

Hypocrite! Writing, being sincere and naked—this isn't possible. Nor is it what I want.

Violent urges, too much violence. I'm not inclined to self-control—though the idea of being a free spirit doesn't attract me either. Since I don't know who I am, I stop at nothing. I have as much boldness and daring as a piece of driftwood. There's always *something* to open my heart. Blood rushes out. Slowly, his Halloween mask on, in comes Death.

Always smiling—it's the Christian's downfall. I don't avoid either pain or wounds. Wounded in my eyes or gut? What I want all the same is strength, not sickness—unwavering strength.

Philosophy's such an easy lay.... And like a "saintly" prankster in bad taste, a friend of shadows. The (sheathed) virility a dog has.

How to be strong enough—and accept—and love??

The dignity of trees (not however when thinking, since thought yearns to be utterly humiliated) and preposterous gentleness. To be with life as you are with a wife, a girlfriend, when making love, drinking, laughing, being attentive, affectionate, even a little eccentric, never purer than when "doing it."

Strength comes from knowing the secret, and the secret's revealed in anguish. A happy child—gurgling, smiling—hasn't the remotest idea of the insomnia of worlds—hasn't an inkling of anguish or ecstasy. The child's good nature keeps these at bay, protects against the worst. A demand must still be made of anguish: don't require the child to give up babbling.

Mine: depression, emptiness, separation, suffering. What I can expect: animal loneliness.

I stared at the walls of my room. My head jerking back.

Suddenly, I *see*. I'd be shouting. As if pulled up out of myself by my own strength, and laughing about it, not able to get my breath. When I say I see, it's screams of fear that see. I'm no longer separated from my death. But if I picture myself alive, survival is my downfall, I stop feeling that I'm choking, I'm unable to see....

In abstinence and austerity there's a shamelessness I enjoy with myself—an aloof, unfriendly coarseness. When I'm feeling free and easy I'm clumsily good-natured, but infinitely gentle and modest. What I hope for is unpretentious asceticism adorning an aloof, gloomy, and unconventional life. Asceticism of this kind couldn't be protected from tidal waves, however, and in every way it would accommodate dangerous excesses.

My endless "trial" makes me long to die....

A kind of radiance and what I suppose is the most violent physical pleasure: I'm a lizard on the wall! In sunlight a state of chaos as its blood spurts out.

At the mercy of chance.... Yesterday I would have spoken only of anguish. Because I *have to* today, I'm bragging of "unflappable lucidity"! There's no rhyme or reason for a change in mood. Animal existence, measured only by the sun and rain, dismissing categories of language.

May/August 1940

2 Solitude

The present time might not be conducive to new truths. The ability to concentrate is weak. The simplest problem—adding numbers—and for a little while I forget what I like most. For other people, time stretches out forever. This is another reason why changing historical conditions monopolize our attention. Prompted to concern for the present and losing sight of the distance, without which the present is ridiculous.

Change and disturbance help give thought the ability to wound, while peaceful times hardly do this. To conquer truth's equivocations, you have to have times that turn people and things upside down, instead of letting them stagnate. From the agony of the mother comes the birth of a child, and we're born in a confusion of sharp cries.

Taking the distant view on the present world (a view taken when someone is dead to it) and seeing it on a scale of waves lapping the centuries *quickly*, you can only be indifferent to the latest that leaves so many human victims clinging helplessly to the litter after the waters recede. You see only the endless succession of buffeting waves as they rise from time's depths, arranging fragile connections, temporary phrases. Only the water's roar is heard as it comes crashing down, pink with blood. The vertigo of the sky and immense movement (only the *immensity* is known) represent, as far as you're concerned (since you can't know their origin or their end), the human nature which is what you are, and which destroys in you all desire for rest. Truly the scene's excessive and it brings disaster with it, leaving you breathless and staggered. But you wouldn't be human until you saw it—innocent until then of admiration that can't repress screams....

It's impossible to know the degree of solitude you'll reach once fate touches you.

The stage when things at last appear *naked* to you is as stifling as the grave. Inevitably *divine impotence* takes you over then—it rips you to pieces, it leaves you in tears.

Laughing, I'm back again, back with other human beings. But their concerns can't reach me any more since when I'm with them I'm blind, deaf. My ability to use things has gone....

For a man, desert dryness and the state of being suspended (suspended from what's around you) are favorable conditions for uprootedness. Nakedness reveals itself when a person is wrapped in hostile solitude. This trial, if difficult, also sets you free; a true state of friendship requires being abandoned by friends, since a free friendship isn't hampered by confining ties. Far beyond the failings of friends and readers I'm close to, I'm now seeking friends and readers a dead person might encounter, and I see them up ahead of me already: innumerable, silent, always true like stars in the heavens. O stars revealed by laughter and folly, my death will join you!

If contentiousness is freed in me, it's so I can be a single point, a foaming edge where the waves' contradictions break up. My awareness (when I'm with others) that I'm a point of rupture and communication again elicits laughter at my suffering and rage. Even if I dismiss this sound and fury, it's mine....

Too many incidents over too long a time *finally* create silence. My sentences seem distant from me—they lack a feeling of being *stifled*. I'd like to stammer today, and I've never been surer of myself. Inside me, the fragmentation of my thinking expresses me only as a play of blinding, secret light.... Think of a man sickened by the laceration I describe...sickened so things wobble for him, so he's on the edge of losing what he ate...someone who can deal with things only when he's drunk...not neurotically drunk, but tipsy in a light-hearted sort of way...while everything spins around him (as if he's about to die)....

With pain like this, you don't make jokes. My willpower's firm, my jaws adequate to the task.... Defying anxiety I recommend my solitude. What would my solitude be without this anxiety—and this anxiety without my solitude?

All our wishes, our expectations, authority, the connections and forms of passionate life, the ownership of property and nations, there's nothing that's not threatened by death, nothing that couldn't vanish tomorrow: the gods themselves in the heights of heaven aren't in less danger of falling from that height than soldiers from dying in a war. Understanding this and having no doubts on this score doesn't provoke either laughter or fear. Mostly, my life is elsewhere.

Going further than I'd gone: last night I seemed to attain growing lucidity and I couldn't sleep. This was distressing, yet as simple as finding something that's lost. Not having it, you're unhappy, but finding it, you're soon bored. Life continued for the rest of that day in me, solid, sure of itself. The idea of having found a certain word seemed empty. I could easily give this word in helpless candor. But the thought of the discovery blocks communication in me. At the moment I'm irritated, discouraged.

Yesterday I consulted a dictionary to find the height of the atmosphere. The weight of the column of air we support apparently is no less than 17 tons. Not far from the word "atmosphere," I paused at Atlixco, a Mexican city at the foot of Popocatepetl (the volcano) in the state of Pueblo. Suddenly I pictured the little town, which I imagine as being like the ones in Southern Andalusia. Buried in oblivion, ignored by the rest of the world, does it continue being itself? It nonetheless continues being what it is—little girls, poverty-stricken women, and maybe in a cluttered room somewhere a boy sobbing and there's sweat running down him.... O world today wracked everywhere with sobs and naively coughing up blood (like a TB victim): on the plains of Poland? Thinking nothing at all would be the same. There's a scream from someone wounded! My solitude is more chaotic than war, and I'm deaf inside it. Even the cries of people on their deathbeds sound empty to me. My solitude is an empire and a struggle goes on for its possession. It's a forgotten star—strong drink and knowledge.

Is the burden I'm taking on too heavy for me, or does my life trifle with every burden and every responsibility? Or are both true: that I

can't escape and that *I'll play*? I can't *not* escape and I can't *not* play.
I'll succeed through rough determination. Refusing the delusions others
live by. My awareness of overcoming them begins to feel like fact. Like
tension that seeks to respond to other tensions. I'm hard and lucid in
my mastery and decisiveness. Too sure of myself to stop where others
can see only failure.

1941

LUCK

1 Sin

The key aspect would be missing still if I didn't speak of sin. Is there anyone who can't comprehend that by proposing sacrifice I've proposed sin as well? Sin is sacrifice, communication is sin. They say sins of the flesh are a sacrifice to Venus. "I consummated a sacrifice of the sweetest kind," as an ancient poet put it. Antiquity's formulation can't be over-looked. And just as love is a sacrifice, sacrifice is a sin. Hubert and Mauss say of the act of putting someone to death: "It's the initial stage of crime, a kind of sacrilege. So, as the victim was led to the place of the murder, certain rituals prescribed libations and expiations...In some cases the murderer was punished—he was beaten or exiled.... The purifications the sacrificer was required to undergo after the sacrifice, moreover, were like the expiations of a criminal" (*Sacrifice*). Respon-sible for the death of Jesus, humankind took on inexpiable crime. This is the apex of sacrifice.

Reading Kierkegaard's *Concept of Dread*. (Dread or anguish.)
For those who understand communication as laceration, communi-cation is sin, or evil. It's a breaking of the established order. Laughter, orgasm, sacrifice (so many failures harrowing the heart) all manifest anguish; in them, a person is anguished, seized and held tight, possessed by anguish. In fact, to be specific, anguish is the serpent, is temptation.

To understand this, three means are necessary: a child's carefree in-difference, the strength of a bull (which is so disappointing in the ring), and the inclination of an ironic bull to linger over the details of his position.

I say: communication is sin. But the opposite is evident! Only self-ishness would be a sin!

The worst thing is the *false light* Blanchot mentions. No one avoids the light glancing off a cobblestone. More formidable is the vague light coming from everywhere (we don't know where from) and coinciding from a certain standpoint with the cobblestone's light. Troubled by false light, a person becomes the victim of reasonable beliefs. He refuses to believe he's abandoned. He's unaware that you have to *recognize* and then *will* abandonment before you can *become* it. And how can he possibly know that the most open means of communication is abandonment? *Truths* keep showing through, they group and regroup in fascinating beams.... They're always changing, but he's always trying to get them to focus. A really intelligent man comes along: he'll focus them in a single beam. Question: will all truth finally disperse when this particular beam regroups? Hardly. The inexhaustible patience of night begins again; the man is healed through forgetting his impotence. Inasmuch as impotence is founded on error, deep down no one desires the light of day: not even Hegel did. Intelligence is directed at a *false light* of day, it wants to grasp some ever-retreating reflection. Daylight would destroy everything, the day would turn into night! Even in me as I write, the work of understanding continues...I'm condemned at least to know what I'm saying. Short of death, there's no way for me to lose myself in this night.

Suppose we take seriously this explanation of conditions under which human existence is communicated: I would then have to *continue* the explaining process. But this can't be done. What's explained eventually changes to its opposite. The most threatening thing about anguish is the convenient construction we put on the truth of this or that particular moment; we're describing only ourselves, perceiving only what seems true to us. If by reason of my coherence I ascribe objectivity to this description, that's inevitable. But I've only displaced the problem. What has changed? What difference does it make if the subject/object connection—namely the one between man and the universe—takes the place of a pure subject? Both the subject and the connection exist. The connection is one of those *false lights*.

I wish intelligence that was as sensitive to pain as teeth are.... It's my lot to have my brains ache, but I'm alone....

Intelligence that understands its ridiculous condition must still explain, according to the laws of explanation, how its condition came to be. Helpless before this last operation, it is, however, no more or less helpless than it is for other questions.

The cohesiveness that a field has inside itself when reduced, the possibility of making reliable predictions, the absolute nature of numbers —to these feeble supports humanity clings like a child to its mother's arms. What meaning would there be in cohesion, in the absolute nature of numbers, if a beyond of another type entirely enclosed them? And what meaning if a beyond wasn't there—if cohesion was everything! If you're unsteady, cohesion and absolutes will only increase your anguish: there's no rest, no certainty, and even non-cohesion's doubtful. The real, the possible, cohesion, and what's beyond cohesion encircle us on all sides, as harassing as an enemy. This is a war without any imaginable peace or truce or hope of victory or defeat.... We call truth definitive and we long for peace, but once again there's war.

I see myself in the night, free of myself. A high mountain rises, a cold wind blows—what can protect you from the wind, from cold, from dark? I'm endlessly climbing a mountainside, teetering as I go. At my feet emptiness yawns: it's bottomless as far as I know. I am emptiness and at the same time the mountaintop, shrouded by night but *present* all the same. My heart's hidden in night like an unpredictable feeling of nausea. I know at sunrise I die.

Little by little, light invades the sky's absence, at first like a feeling of discomfort. Time goes by and the discomfort nauseates me...day breaks. I understand that in nausea my heart hides a sun, a sun I now detest. Slowly the sun rises into light. As I die, no sound breaks from my mouth, for the cry I give is a silence without end.

Christians refuse to understand the childishness of their attitudes, their lack of manliness before God. If (and only if) we reject God are we manly. It's on this basis, not on theological abstractions, that the definition of the word God depends.

Hearing a priest's voice on the radio, so childish, so humble, which is acceptable behavior only for a priest.

Contrary to what's usually admitted, language isn't communication but its negation, at least its relative negation—as with the telephone (or radio).

Thought and morality can only be impoverishment if there's no glorification of the nakedness of an attractive whore intoxicated from having a male organ in her.* Turning away from her glory is averting your eyes from the sun.

Intellectual toughness, seriousness and the will tensed in surrender. Total manliness. Putting a distance between yourself and kindness, pity, the softer feelings—or between yourself and intellectual life anyway. It doesn't matter that a whore *has to* be beautiful or that her behavior leads to her ruin.

The fact that we can't persevere in lust, that we meet only chance outlines and then are pushed back and, next, pay with endless worry for any pleasure we experience, points out how unfavorable lust is to integrity. But to the extent that the integrity of a person is a harmony in the succession of time, you have to admit a will to harmony leads to illusory negation. It leads to camouflaging *what is*.

In my concern for other people I'm a little like the parish priest! If a woman's on the decline, I'm heartless and can't abide either the woman or her decline!

The pride (presumption) of some involves those who come later. Knowledge implies chronically going astray. I consider the succession of changing thoughts to be a single interdependent movement. When deviation begins, you have to submit to its consequences, you can't refuse pride. Even the complete straying of non-knowledge (falling into night) requires proud assurance. Should I improperly justify my pride by saying that the pride of others is improper?

Nietzsche's principle ("It's false if it doesn't make you laugh at least once") is at the same time associated with laughter and with *ecstatic loss of knowledge*.

* In the 1944 edition I had to substitute suspension points for two words. [1960 Note].

2 Games of Chance

Pain shaped my character. In school, with my frostbitten fingers—pain is the teacher. "Without your pain, you're nothing!"

Tears in my eyes at this idea of being waste! I'm whining, ready to pray, but just can't make myself.

A moment later I'm clenching and unclenching my teeth, and drowsiness sets in.

A toothache strikes, my brain turns to mush.

I'm writing and appealing—but hoping for relief from the pain makes me feel that much worse.

Knowing nothing about the creature I am or what kind of thing I am—is there anything I do know? At night not being able to go on and banging my head against the wall, trying to find a way, not from self-confidence but because of being sentenced to search, bumping into things, bleeding, falling down, not getting up.... Feeling I can't go on, aware of pincers torturing my fingers, of red-hot branding irons burning the soles of my feet. Where is the way out, except for pincers and branding irons! No compromise and no escape. In actuality I'm *safe* from them?! At least they'd confer legitimacy on my body. Which can't *in truth* be separated from them. Which can't be separated from them *in truth*. (You can't separate the body from the head either.)

What if this urgent pain finally didn't matter? At least I'd have some hope of rest. Thinking stops for me, I'm in sunlight, no more worry. How is it possible that earlier I had moments of total well-being on the banks of rivers, in woods, gardens, cafes, in my room? (Leaving aside the darker joys.)

A slipping, glance down, the molar's extracted, but the anesthetic isn't working? What an awful experience!

What would it be like, how big a coward would I have been, without the hope the cocaine gave? When I get home, I bleed profusely. I stick my tongue in the hole…there's a piece of meat there, a blood clot getting larger, starting to protrude. I spit it out—another follows. The clots have the consistency of snot, taste like food gone bad. They're plugging up my mouth. I decide that by falling asleep I'll get over my disgust, won't be tempted to fuss with them or spit them out. I drift off and wake up at the end of an hour.… Blood streamed from my mouth in my sleep, stained the pillow and sheet, and there are clots stuck in the sheet-folds, almost dry, some black like snot. I'm still upset and exhausted. I'm picturing an incident of hemophilia, maybe followed by death (is that so impossible?). I don't want to die. Or maybe what I mean is—to hell with death. My disgust grows. I put a basin at the foot of the bed to avoid getting up during the night to spit in the toilet. In the coal stove, the fire's gone out and the thought of having to start it again depresses me. I can't get back to sleep.… Time drags on. Sometimes I get drowsy. At 5 or 6 in the morning I decide to light the fire. I might as well make some use of this insomnia and get a thankless job out of the way. The ashes from the stove have to be taken out. I do the job badly, and soon the room's strewn with pieces of coal, clinkers, and ashes. The enamel basin is filled with blood, it's dirty with it, and with clots, the blood has made puddles on my filthy sheets. Exhausted by insomnia, I'm still bleeding and the snotty taste of the clots gets more and more disgusting all the time. Finally the fire catches. My hands black with coal and dirty with blood. Blood-caked lips. A thick coal smoke fills the room; as usual, it takes a huge effort to get the resistant coal to catch fire. I'm not impatient, and no more anguished than other days. There's a nagging need in me…to rest.

Little by little the uproar, hearty laughter, and songs disappeared in the distance. The bow still drew out its dying note which continued with diminished strength and finally disappeared like an indistinct sound in the vastness of the atmosphere. At times a rhythmic shock was heard on the road, something that resembled the distant roar of the sea, then nothing, nothing but emptiness and silence.

And isn't it in some way like this that happiness—a guest as delightful

as he is fickle—slips away from us, and then how vainly does isolated
sound claim to express joy! For in its own echo it can't hear anything
but melancholy and loneliness, and how pointlessly we insist on lend-
ing our ear to it.

Gogol, *Nights in the Ukraine*

We can't *know* if humanity is generally good luck or bad. The fact
that we confine ourselves to polemical truth shows ambiguous judgment, tying good luck to what we are and bad luck to the curse em-
bodied by the wicked. In contrast, clear judgment welcomes the fact of
evil and the warfare of good against evil (the incurable wound of being).
With ambiguous judgment, however, merit isn't conditional; and good
(which we are) isn't luck but a thing we deserve. It's being's answer to
the necessity of being, everything appearing planned out in advance,
"cooked up," arranged, it seems, by a God whose ends we can't
question.

The human mind is set up to take no account of chance, except insofar as the calculations that eliminate chance allow you to forget it:
that is, *not take it into account.* But going as far as possible, reflection
on chance strips the world bare of the entirety of predictions in which
reason encloses it. Like human nakedness, the nakedness of chance—
which in the last resort is definitive—is obscene and disgusting: in short,
divine. Since the course of the things of the world hangs on chance, this
course is as depressing for us as a king's absolute power.

My reflections on chance are *in the margin of* thought's development.
All the same, we can't make them more radical (decisive). Descending
as far as possible, they pull the rug out from under us when we think
that the development of thought allows sitting down, allows rest.

A part of what applies to us can be—must be—reduced to reason or
(through knowledge or science) to systematic understanding. We can't
suppress the fact that at one point everything and every law was decided
according to the whims of chance—or *luck*—without reason entering
the picture, except when the calculation of probabilities allowed it to.

It's true, the omnipotence of reason limits luck's power. This limi-
tation in principle suffices, and in the long run the course of the world
obeys law. And since we're rational we see this; but the course of things
escapes us at the extremes.

At the extremes, there's freedom.

At the extremes, thought ceases to be!

At least within the limits of possibilities that pertain to us, thought can only be present in two ways:

1) Thought is allowed to catch sight of and (in fascination) meditate on the open expanses of catastrophe. The calculus of probabilities limits the scope of this catastrophe, but as death makes us subjects of its empire, the meaning (or non-meaning) of catastrophe isn't to that extent "humanly" cancelled.

2) Part of human life escapes from work and reaches freedom. This is the part of play that is controlled by reason, but, within reason's limits, determines the brief possibilities of a leap beyond those limits. Play, which is as fascinating as catastrophe, allows you to positively glimpse *the giddy seductiveness of chance.*

I grasp the object of my desire. I tie myself to this object, live in it. It's as sure as light, and like the first hesitant star in the night sky, it's a marvel. In order to know this object with me, someone would have to accommodate my darkness. This distant object is unfamiliar, but familiar too—every flowery exhalation of a young girl, the hectic flush of her cheeks touches it. And it's so transparent a breath will tarnish it, a word dissipate it.

A man betrays chance in a million ways, and in a million ways he betrays "what he is." Can you claim you'll never give in to repressive frowning rigidity? The mere fact of not giving in is itself a betrayal. In the fabric of chance, dark interlinks with light. It was only to pursue and mutilate me on a path to horror, depression, and denial (as well as to license and excess) that chance touched me in airy lightness, in utter weightlessness (slow down, dawdle, grow sluggish even for an instant, and chance will disappear). I'd have never found it by looking. Speaking, I've surely betrayed it already. Only if I don't care about betraying myself or about other people's betrayal of me do I escape treachery. I'm dedicated to chance with everything in me, my whole life, all my strength—and there's only absence and inanity in me...laughter, such *light* laughter! Chance: I imagine, in the gloom of night, a knife-tip entering my heart, a happiness beyond limits, unbearable happiness....

> *the light too much joy too much heaven too much*
> *the earth too vast a fast-moving horse*
> *I hear the waters I'm weeping for light*

the earth turns beneath my eyelids
stones roll in my bones
the anemone and glow-worm
help me to unconsciousness

in a shroud of roses
an incandescent teardrop
proclaims the day.

Two opposing impulses seek out chance. One of these is predatory, inducing dizziness; the other promotes harmony. One requires
violent sexual union—bad luck sinks voraciously on luck, consumes it
or at least abandons it and marks it with the sign of doom. There's a
flaring up and bad luck takes its course, ending in death. The other is
divination, the wish to read chance, be its reflection, be lost in its light.
Mostly the opposing movements reach an understanding, each with
the other. But if we seek the kind of harmony that's found in turning
away from violence, chance is cancelled out as such, it's set on a regular and monotonous path. Chance arises from disorder, not regular-
ity. It demands randomness—its light sparkles in dark obscurity. We
fail it when we shield it from misfortune, and its sparkle abandons it
when failed.

Chance is more than beauty, but beauty derives its sparkle from
chance.
The huge majority (bad luck) drags beauty down to prostitution.

All chance is sullied. Beauty can't exist without a flaw. Perfect, chance
and beauty have stopped being what they are: they're the rule. The desire for chance is inside us like a sore tooth, and at the same time it's
the opposite—it wants misfortune's unfocused coziness.

The consummation of chance in a burst of lightning and the fall that
follows the consummation can't be—painlessly—imagined by anyone.

The gossamer-like lacerating idea of chance!

Chance is hard to bear. Commonly it's destroyed and the bottom of
things drops out. Chance wants to be *impersonal* (or it's vanity, a bird
in a cage), hard to put your hands on, melancholy, slipping out into
night like a song....

I can't imagine a *spiritual* way of life that isn't impersonal, dependent on chance, never on efforts of the will.

On a roof I saw large, sturdy hooks* placed halfway up. Suppose someone falls from a rooftop…couldn't he maybe *catch hold* of one of those hooks with an arm or leg? If I fell from a rooftop, I'd plummet to the ground. But if a hook was there, I'd come to a stop halfway down!

Just a little later I might say to myself: "Once an architect planned this hook, and without it I'd be dead. I should be dead, but I'm not at all—in fact, I'm alive. A hook was put there."
Let's say my presence, my life are inescapable. Something impossible and incomprehensible would still be its principle.

I understand now—picturing the momentum of falling—that there's nothing in this world unless it meets up with a *hook*.

Usually we avoid seeing a hook. We confer an aspect of necessity on ourselves, on the universe, on the earth, on people.

With a hook arranging the universe, I plunged into an infinite play of mirrors. This play had the same principle as a fall blocked by a hook. Can anyone get more into the core of things? I shook. I couldn't go on. Rapture within me, emotion welling up to the point of tears, rituals of darkness that defy description, every orgy in the world and all times blending in this light.

Do I have it in me to say it? It hardly matters. Since chance has again been given to me, so has rapture—to the point that in a sense it never stopped. Sometimes, though rarely, I feel a need to remind myself of the fact. But this is from weakness. Sometimes from the indifference that comes from utter impurity or in the expectation of death.

There was anguish in me because every value was chance, and its existence and my ability to find it depended on chance. A value was when X number of people agreed, and when chance was each person's motivation and when chance—the chance that existed in their affirmation—brought them to agree (this chance could only *after the fact* be called will or calculation). I pictured this chance not in mathe-

* [Hooks like these are used to hold poles on the roofs to prevent snow from sliding off in the winter. TR.]

matical form but as a key that could bring being into harmony with whatever surrounded it, since being is itself harmony, a harmony with what chance *is* in the first place. A light is destroyed in the depths of the possibility of being. Being is destroyed and breath is suspended; it's reduced to a feeling of silence, so that there's a harmony there which is completely improbable. Strokes of luck wager being, successively enrich (human) being with the potentiality to harmonize with luck, with the power of revealing or creating luck (since luck is the art of being, or being is the art of welcoming and loving luck). There's no great distance from anguish to a feeling of bad luck to harmony. Anguish is necessary to harmony, bad luck to luck, a mother's insomnia to a child's laughter.

Value not based on chance would be arguable.

Ecstasy is linked to knowledge. I enter ecstasy looking for the manifest or obvious, for a value that isn't arguable and is given in advance, but which, from powerlessness and impotence, I couldn't ever find. What might finally be the object of my knowing answers the question of my anguish. Let me prophesy: in the end I will say and know "what is."

If the will to anguish can only *ask* questions, the answer, if it comes, wills that anguish be maintained. The answer is, anguish is your fate. How could a person like you know what you are or what is...or anything? Alone in escaping definitive checkmate are platitude, deception, and the trickery of those who are anguished.

In a certainty of impotence, anguish stops asking questions, or all its questions remain hopeless. Chance impulse never asks questions and to this end makes use of the opposite impulse, anguish, its accomplice, which it adopts and without which it would perish.

Chance is an effect of gambling. This effect can never come to rest. Wagered again and again, chance is a *misunderstanding* of anguish (to the extent that anguish is a desire for rest, for satisfaction). This impulse leads to the only real end of anguish—the absence of an answer. It's an impulse that can never overcome anguish, for in order to be chance and nothing other than chance, the movement of chance has to *desire* that anguish will subsist and chance remain wagered.

If it didn't stop along the way, art would exhaust the movement of chance. It would become something else and more.* Chance, though,

* In fact, art escapes. On principle artists mostly limit themselves to their specialty. If they exceed it, it's sometimes to further a truth that's even more important in their eyes than art itself. Most artists refuse to see that art encourages them to create a god-like (in our times, a God-like) world.

isn't capable of dawdling, and its lightness of foot protects it from this "more." It wants to have its success incomplete and quickly emptied of meaning, one success is soon left behind for another. Hardly does the success appear than its light is extinguished, and another is called forth. Success wants to be gambled, gambled again, wagered endlessly whenever the cards are dealt in a new game.

Personal luck hasn't much to do with luck. Mostly it's a sorry blend of conceit and anguish. Chance is only chance provided that impersonality, or a game of communication that never ends, can be glimpsed.

The light of chance is dimmed by artistic success. As a matter of fact, chance is a woman who wants to be undressed.

Bad luck or anguish sustains the possibility of luck. The same cannot be said of vanity or reason (or, generally, of whatever impulses lead a person to give up playing—gambling, that is).

A fleeting, stifling beauty, embodying chance in a woman's body, is attained through love. But possession of chance requires fingers as light as chance itself. You have to have fingers that don't grasp. Nothing is more contrary to chance (to love) than endless questioning or anxious trembling or the need to exclude unfavorable chance developments; nothing is more pointless than exhausting reflection. I come to love with an enchanted lack of concern, which in its folly is the reverse of a lack of concern. Ponderousness excludes passion so thoroughly you might as well not consider it. In its singlemindedness, love is weakness, melodrama, a need to suffer. Chance summons a chaos through which its links are forever and continuously forged. Affectation, a closed mind, and conventional love feelings represent a negation *in spite of which* love is intense, passionate (but we reply to chance by *intentionally* setting the odds against ourselves).

—Even momentarily, ponderousness is a destruction of chance.—All philosophy (all of knowledge makes chance into an exception) is reflection on a lifeless residue, on a regular process that allows neither chance nor mischance. To recognize chance* is a suicide of knowledge, and chance, concealed in a philosopher's despair, bursts out in the frothings of the demented.—I base my conviction on the folly of my fellow human beings (or on the intensity of my pleasure). If I hadn't previously exhausted and measured the possibilities of the mind, turning them upside down, what would I have to say? One day I'll *try chance*

* This has nothing to do with a calculus of probabilities. [1959 Note]

out, and, moving across eggs like a sprite, I'll let it be understood I'm walking, and my wisdom will seem magical. Possibly this excludes other people—assuming that my attaining chance demands *knowing nothing about them*! Man reads the possible outline of chance in his "customs," an outline that is himself, a state of grace, an arrow let fly. Animals were a wager, and so is man, we're an arrow released into air. Where it will fall, I can't say. Where I'll fall, I can't say.

What is more frightening for humankind than play?

Humanness can't stop halfway. But I'm wrong to say *humanness....* A human being is also the opposite of a human being—the endless questioning of what his name designates!

You can only oppose mischance's tumultuous act of consuming chance by yielding to the greed for chance. Greed is more opposed to chance—and ruins it more completely—than the tumultuous event of a storm. Tumult reveals chance's nature, showing it nakedly and breathing it out like fever. In the equivocal glare of tumult, the cruelty of chance, its impurity, and the perverse meaning of chance appear as they are, adorned in sovereign magic.

With women, chance can be seen in signs readable on the lips, kisses that recall moments of deadly tumultuousness.

In principle, death is opposed to chance. Still, chance is sometimes linked to its opposite: so death could be the mother of chance.

On the other hand, chance (which differs in this way from mathematical scarcity) is defined by the will it fulfills. Willpower can't be indifferent to the chance it summons up. We couldn't think of will without the chance that accomplishes it—nor of chance without the willpower that seeks it out.

Willpower negates death, it's even unconcerned with it. Only anguish produces concern for death, paralyzing the will. The will relies on the certainty of chance and is the opposite of the fear of death. Will guesses what chance is and fixes it: it's an arrow that moves towards it. Chance and will unite in love. Love hasn't any object but chance, and only chance has the strength to love.

Chance is forever at the mercy of itself. It's always at the mercy of play, always *in* play. If it was definitive, chance wouldn't be chance. And reciprocally, if there was definitive being in the world, there'd be no more chance (the chance in it would be dead).

Irrational faith and chance flare-ups attract chance. Chance is given in a living state of heat, not in an outside, objective randomness. Chance is a state of grace, a gift of heaven, permission to roll the dice without any possibility of repetition, without anguish.

The attractions of completion come from its inaccessible character. The habit of cheating adorns definitive being in chance apparel.

This morning a sentence of mine lacerated me, "With women, chance can be seen.... " Only the way mystics depict *their* condition can correspond to my laceration.

There's no room for doubt now: intelligence must apprehend chance if it's to limit itself to its own domain, that is action. Similarly, chance is an object of human ecstasy, because it's the opposite of a response to the desire to know.

THE OBJECT OF ECSTASY IS THE ABSENCE OF AN OUTSIDE ANSWER. THE INEXPLICABLE PRESENCE OF MAN IS THE ANSWER THE WILL GIVES ITSELF SUSPENDED IN THE VOID OF UNKNOWABLE NIGHT. THIS NIGHT, THROUGH AND THROUGH, HAS THE SHAMELESSNESS OF A ROOF-HOOK.

The will grasps the fact of its own conflagration, discerns within itself an aspect which is dream-like, a shooting star which night can't grasp.

From chance to poetry, the distance derives from the inanity of so-called poetry. A calculated use of words, the negation of poetry, destroys chance and reduces things to what they are. Using words poetically involves a perversion akin to the hellish beauty of faces or bodies—which death reduces to nothing.

The absence of poetry is the eclipse of chance.
Chance is like death: "the harsh embrace of a lover, desired, feared." Chance is the painful place of overlap of life and death—in sex and in ecstasy, in laughter and in tears.

Chance has the power to love death. But this desire destroys death too (less certainly than hatred of death or fear of it). The path to chance is hard to follow; it's threatened by, but also inseparable from, horror and death. Without horror and death or without the *risk* of them, where would the magic of chance be?

"Every flowery exhalation of a young girl, the hectic flush of her cheek touches it. And it's so transparent a breath will tarnish it, a word dissipate it." To discern the audacity of play with each passing impulse—but I'm prevented from this by anguish. In anguish a flower withers...life reeks of death.

Life is the folly of rolling dice without another thought—the insistence on a state of grace, on lack of consequences. To worry about consequences is the beginning of greed and anguish. The latter comes from the former: it's the trembling produced by chance. Often anguish punishes greed in its initial stages, drawing it on to its more developed perversion, anguish.

In a general way, religion *questions everything*. And particular religions are structures that create the particular responses. Sheltered by these structures, unlimited questioning takes place. But the question to be answered subsists in its entirety, untouched by the history of the particular religions. The uneasiness, deep-seated, has remained while the answers have dissipated.

The answers are lucky or unlucky throws of the dice, and life has been wagered on these. It's even true the wagering of life has been so innocent that combinations of the dice can't be perceived as results of chance. But only wagering was the truth of the response. The response caused a renewal of the game, maintained the questioning, the wagering. Withdrawal of the response, though, is a second aspect of this.

But if a response is chance, the questioning won't stop and the stakes are still untouched: the response is the questioning itself.

Chance calls up *spiritual* life—the highest stakes. In traditional contacts with chance (from card playing to poetry), we only skim the surface. (As I write this, it happens that I feel chance's searing hand abruptly pulling me up—wrenching me out of the bed where I'm writing this—leaving me paralyzed. I can't speak except of the necessity of loving chance to the point of giddiness, and of how far chance withdraws, in this understanding, from what my vulgarity took it to be!)

Nothing goes as violently beyond *understanding*'s limits. At a pinch we can imagine utmost intensity, beauty, and nakedness. But not at all a being endowed with speech, not at all God, a sovereign lord....

Just a few minutes later my memory is already shaky. A vision like this can't be fit into the world. It's related to this statement: "What is present, but demented, all the same is *impossible*." *What is present* is fragility itself (God is the foundation)! In any case it's what couldn't not have been.

Intellectual curiosity puts chance beyond my reach. I seek it and it escapes, as if I just missed it.

Though once again.... This time I've seen it as *a light shining through*. As if nothing existed except in this clarity—suspended from a roof-hook. Nothing except what possibly might not have been, what possibly should not have been...nothing except what dies and is consumed and wagered. This *shining through* came to me in a new light— a precarious, questionable light that couldn't be, except *at that cost*.

A sunset sky dazzles me and fills me with wonder...but that doesn't make it a living being.
Imagine the incomparable beauty of a woman who happens to be dead. She's not a living being, there's nothing to be understood about her. No one's in the bedroom. God's not. The room's empty.

To be an arrow is the nature of chance. This particular arrow, one that's different from the rest, and only *my* heart is wounded. If I fall down and die and it's this arrow at last, it's this and not another. It is what it is, thanks to the power of my heart; it's stopped being distinct from me.

How can you *recognize* chance unless you're filled with secret love for it?
An insane love creates it, hurling itself at your face in silence. And chance fell on me from heaven's heights like a bolt from the blue—and chance was who I am! A tiny drop shattered by the bolt, a brief moment shines brighter than the sun.

In front of me and inside me there's no God, no separate being, but flickering *connections*.

Laughter on my lips, as I *recognize* chance on them. Chance!

"*I'm probably doomed,*" *mused Thomas.* "*I don't have the strength to wait any longer. Even if I thought I could overcome my weakness a little longer as long as I wasn't alone—now there's no reason to keep making efforts. It's obviously depressing to get so close to the goal and not be able to touch it. I'm sure if I reached those last steps I'd understand why I've struggled uselessly looking for something I haven't found. This is rotten luck, and I'm dying of it.*"

"*It's only in this last room, located at the top of the house, that night will completely unfold. Usually it's lovely and peaceful. It's a relief not to have to shut your eyes to get rid of daytime's insomnia. It's also rather seductive to find in outer darkness the same night that for such a long time struck your inner truth with death. This night has a very special nature. It's not accompanied either by dreams or by premonitory thoughts that are sometimes substituted for dreams. It's a vast dream itself which, if it covers you, you never attain. When at last it swathes your bed, we'll draw the curtains around you and the splendor of the objects revealed at that point will be worthy of consoling even those who are unhappiest. At that instant I'll become really beautiful myself. This false light makes me rather unattractive now, but at that auspicious moment I'll appear as I actually am. I'll look at you for a long time and I'll lie down close to you—and you won't need to ask about things, I'll answer all your questions. Also—and at the same time—the lamps whose inscriptions you wanted to read will be turned around so they face the right way, and wise sayings that allow everything to be understood will no longer be illegible. So don't be impatient. The night will render you justice, and you'll lose sight of all sorrow and fatigue.*"

"*One last question,*" *said Thomas after listening with lively interest.* "*Will the lamps be lit?*"

"*Of course not,*" *the girl said.* "*What a ridiculous question! Everything will be lost in the night.*"

"*The night,*" *Thomas said in a dreamy way.* "*So I won't see you?*"

"*Most likely not,*" *said the girl.* "*Did you think it would be different from this? It's precisely because you'll be lost forever in darkness and you won't be able to perceive anything yourself that I'm telling you about it now. You can't expect to hear, see and be at rest all at once. So I'm letting you know what will happen when night reveals its truth to you while you're deeply at rest. Doesn't it please you to know that in a short time everything you've wanted to learn will be read in a few*

straightforward words on the walls, on my face and on my mouth? Now
the fact that this revelation won't actually be disclosed to you, to be
honest, is a drawback, but the main thing is to be sure you won't have
struggled in vain. Picture for a minute how it will be. I'll take you in
my arms and the words I'll murmur in your ear will have such incredible
importance that, if you heard them, you'd be transformed. And my face!
My deepest wish is for you to see it then, since at that moment—and not
a minute sooner—you'll recognize me. And you'll know whether you've
found the person you believe you've been searching for during your jour-
neys, the person for whom miraculously you came to this house—mi-
raculously, but pointlessly. Think of the joy it would be! More than any-
thing, you've desired to see her again. Arriving at this place, which is so
hard to enter, you thought at last the goal was near and that the worst
was behind you. Oh how you stuck with memory! It was extraordinary,
I admit. Others totally forget their former life when they arrive. But
you've kept a small memory inside, a weakened signal you've not al-
lowed to fail. Of course, since you've allowed many memories to become
indistinct, for me it's as if thousands of miles separated us. I can hardly
make you out. It's difficult for me to imagine that one day I'll know who
you are. But soon, very soon we'll finally be united. I'll open my arms
and throw them around you—and I'll move with you through deep se-
crets. We'll lose—then find—each other. Nothing will ever come between
us again. It's sad you won't be present for this happiness!"

Maurice Blanchot, *Aminadab*

To wager or question "self."

When a person pursues a minor object he's not questioning *himself*
(questioning "self" would be suspended then). To love a minor object
—even when the object is a concatenation of lacerating words—hinders
laceration (unless the laceration is attained and your sentence, no
longer an object but a transition, becomes the expression of *laceration*).

Insanely loving chance, you wager everything...even reason itself.
When the power of speech comes into the picture, the limit of possibility
is the only limit.

Currently a human being's chance results from the play of natural or
physiological factors (the lucky dimensions of humankind are intellectual, psychological, or physical). Acquiring chance is what's at stake
when constantly questioning yourself.

But chance is finally purified. It's freed from minor objects and is reduced to its own inner nature. Chance no longer is a solitary lucky response (among many) to the simple fact of risk. In the end the response is chance itself—gambling, endlessly putting questions. Finally chance is a wagering of all possibilities and it *depends* on that wagering (so it's not *distinct* from it any more).

If Good didn't question itself it would be the judge's power of execution.
Take Good out of the picture, even for a minute, and you end up kissing the hem of the judge's robe.

Good and its retainers breathe the air exhaled by murderers—they kiss the muddy footprints of killers.

If I say Good risks anything, I'm giving dead stone a living heart.

In me, the living idea of *Good* has a function like "a man holding onto a roof-hook." It depends on some random "hook." Isolated from the pitch of the roof, from slipping, from tumbling down, the idea of Good is frozen. Everything's always moving. If I get an idea, I wager it—and motion's imparted.

God discloses the horror of a world where there is constant risk and nothing is protected. In fact, the opposite is true. The multitude of random beings corresponds with the possibility that things are always in play. If God existed (if he unchangeably was once and for all) the possibility of play would disappear at the pinnacle.

When I'm not my choice of love object any more, I love a gray cloud...and gray heavens. In flight from me, chance is in free play in the heavens. The heavens—which obliquely link me even with beings of the future. How could the issue, or problem, of the multitude of individual beings be tolerable?

Haunted by the idea of knowing what the key to the mystery is, a man becomes a reader of detective novels. Still, could the universe resemble calculations worked out by writers to evoke recognizable worlds?
There's no explanation and *the mystery has no key*. There's nothing conceivable outside "appearance," and the desire to escape appearance ends up switching appearances: we're in no way closer to the truth *that*

isn't. Outside appearance, there's nothing. Or outside appearance, *there's night.* And: in the night there's only the night. If at night there was anything that could be expressed by using language, this would be night all the same. Being itself can be reduced to appearance or doesn't exist. Being is the absence that appearances conceal.

Night is richer, as a representation, than being is. Chance comes from night, returns to night—it is both daughter and mother of night. Night doesn't exist, and neither does chance. Chance, since it *is* what *isn't*, reduces being to the deposing of chance (chance, now removed from the game, searches for substance). Being, Hegel says, is the most impoverished notion. Chance, I say, is the richest. Chance—by which being is destroyed in its beyond.

What I call gambling is the world seen from the night of unknowing. Which is different from *laws* obeyed by the world as it's gambled.

Truths wagered like instances of chance, gambled on the lie of being—these truths are wagered and then wagered again. The truths that express being have a need *not* to change—to be changeless.

What does it mean if you say, "I could have been him or her"? To put it less maniacally, "What if I was God?" A definitive distribution of being—guaranteed by God who himself is distinct from other people—doesn't terrify me any less than emptiness as soon as I fall into it. God can't just forget or annihilate the differences we long for. It's obvious he's their negation! (God wouldn't be subject to distribution.) *God is not me*: that proposition makes me laugh until, all alone at night, I stop laughing, and, being alone, I'm lacerated by my unrestrained laughter. "Why am I not God?" From my childishness comes the answer—"I'm me." But, "Why am I who I am?" "If I wasn't myself, would I be God?" The terror is rising in me, since—what do *I* know anyway? And catching hold of the drawer-handle I squeeze tight with my finger-bones. What if God started wondering, "Why am I myself?" or "Why not be this person who is writing?" Or…"*Somebody*, anyway!" Do I have to draw the conclusion that "God's a person who doesn't question himself, a *self* who knows the reasons he is who he is"? When I act dumb, I resemble him. How true is this? I'd be terrified *to be him* right now. Only humility makes my powerlessness bearable. If I were all-powerful….

God is dead. He's so dead, in fact, that the only way to make this comprehensible is by killing myself.

The normal development of knowledge limits me to myself. It convinces me that the world ends with me. But I can't dwell on that connection. I stray, I evade and neglect myself, and I find it impossible to return to an attachment to self except through taking up a neglectful attitude. I live only by neglecting myself, I care about myself only provided I'm alive.

The beloved self! I see him now, devoted, familiar, romping around. No doubt about it—that's *him*! But the old dog doesn't care about being taken that seriously any more. Under certain circumstances and in a spirit of fun, he might opt for the somewhat eccentric doggy role that shows up in stories, or, when feeling down, be a doggy ghost.

Before I was born—you might ask—what were my chances of coming into this world? I'm alluding to times my family experienced. I'm imagining meetings without which I wouldn't be. The chances of their taking place were *that infinitely small*.

The big lie: existing in this world under these conditions and thinking up a God who's like us! A God who calls himself *me*!

Imagine a God—a being distinct from others—calling himself *I*, though this I never occurred and doesn't result from occurrence. This kind of nonsense transposes a notion we have of ourselves onto a scale of totality. God is the kind of impasse that happens when the world (which simultaneously destroys both us and whatever exists) surrounds our *self* to give it the illusion of possible salvation. Self then blends the giddy prospects of ceasing to exist with the dreams we have of escaping death.
Once we return to straightforwardness, the God of theology is only a response to a nagging urge of the self to be finally *taken out of play*.

Theology's God, reason's god, is never brought into play. The unbearable self we are comes into play endlessly. "Communication" brings it into play endlessly.

Occurrence itself—or origin—is "communication," sperm and egg slide into each other in the heart of the sexual storm.

Chance wagers people as they join—when two by two or in larger groupings they sometimes dream, act, make love, curse, dominate, and kill each other.

Before conjunction, a man forgets about himself—he's drawn to his beloved. Like rain raining or thunder thundering, in this tumultuous conjunction a child occurs.

In sacrifice, mischance "tempestuously consumes chance," designating a priest "with the sign of disaster" (making him sacred). Nonetheless, the priest is not chance, but uses mischance for the purposes of chance. In other words, chance, consumed by mischance, sometimes is chance in its origin and result. That, apparently, is the secret of chance; it can be discovered only when being gambled away. But the best way to gamble it away is to destroy it.

Prostitutes and organs of pleasure are marked with "the sign of disaster." Mischance is a drinking glass filled with horrible fluid—I have to put my finger inside. How otherwise could I receive chance's discharge? Laughter and thunder are wagered in me. But hardly do I withdraw, exhausted from the horrible game, than the storm (or a crash I dream about, or a heart attack) is replaced by a vulgar feeling of emptiness.

At a time of confusion and anxiety when I searched frantically for something to link me to chance, I still had to kill time. I didn't want to give in to the cold then. To keep from giving in, I intended to find consolation in a book. But available books were ponderous, hostile, too stilted—except for poems of Emily Brontë.

That inconceivable creature answered…

Heaven's great laughter bursts on our heads
earth never misses Absence.

She spoke of a time

when his fine golden hair
would tangle roots of grass beneath the ground.

1942/1943

THE DIVINITY OF LAUGHTER

1 Occurrence

If man's an occurrence, what occurs isn't the answer to a question—it's the occurrence of a question. We ask questions and can't close a wound opened by hopeless questioning in us: *"Who am I? What am I?"*

I am—man is—a calling into question of what we are, of individual being wherever it is—a limitless calling into question, or being, insofar as it becomes self-questioning.

Does occurrence insofar as it occurs (insofar as, possibly, it might not have occurred as such) have self-questioning as its end? The possibly infinite number of different answers (in place of the answer which the occurrence is—the other answers not having occurred nor ever being able to do so) maintains the nature of occurrence as questioning. Each occurrence (each individual being) is the outcry of a questioning, an affirmation of a randomness or *contingency*. But man's more than this: there's questioning in us and it's not just the kind of questioning that there is in stars (or microorganic life). We conjugate all the modes of questioning in the forms of our consciousness, finally becoming (reducing ourselves to) a questioning that doesn't have an answer.

As occurrence, man is an occurrence of questioning as questioning becomes subjective being (tending towards an autonomy in nature and so being conceived of in laughter).

The ultimate development of knowledge is questioning. We can't endlessly defer to answers...to knowledge...and knowledge finally opens a void. At the summit of knowledge, knowledge stops. I yield, and everything's vertigo.

2 The Need For Laughter

I always withdrew from occurrence, afraid of being *what I was*—
LAUGHTER ITSELF!

Slowly, fever.... Darkness growing, a world is giving birth to something, veins are standing out on my temples, this cold sweat.... Eyes
inflamed, mouth dry, a queasiness pushing up words from my throat,
I choke. I didn't turn my eyes away (sometimes, though, I wanted
to...).

A's good luck insults B's *lack* of it. Or else luck gets ashamed and
hides. Constricting waves of sickly sickness—I'm at the core of it.

If I laugh now, maybe unbearable pain will be the cost. I can laugh
from a core of unhappiness. Or I can laugh because I'm suspended by
chance.

Oh if I could *die* from this laughing!... Today dying isn't any big deal.
What's clear is—the last act isn't easy. What else is there to say?

On the plane of impossibility, I love Poe and Baudelaire and I burn
with *their* fire. Will I have more strength than they do—*more
consciousness*?

Poe and Baudelaire measured impossibility like children. Like Don
Quixote. Or like being *white with fear*.

"Recover your willpower before rats gnaw it away!"

My will: relaxing out in sunlight, in shade, reading, a little wine (my appetite for rich, hot food), the hazy empty sun-drenched countryside, writing, putting notes into book form (a goal that requires self-discipline from me, self-control competing with my easy-going side, my childishness: something has to shake me out of complacency). I suggest to myself that we come to terms, that we reach an agreement.

My will: a stream that flows along. I'm hardly a man. Defended by my teeth? I'm yawning to prove brilliantly…(what?)…I'm dreaming. I flow along unaware of who I am, except that I get drunk, put others in a similar condition.

There's nothing I can possess, that's clear (all the same I still have to eat and drink, sometimes not do anything at all, and that's where hazard or chance comes in…what would I do without chance?).

Huge randomness.

An alternation (between a stream flowing along and the eagle over the waters). Twistings, turnings. The countryside can't be described, tree-studded, various, made of conflict and "pleasantness." Everything in it disconcerting. Uneasiness succeeded by relaxation. Like an excited dog that circles, appearing and disappearing. I'm speaking of laughter.

To the right is a gable made of hollow bricks. Big buzzy insect crawling inside one of the bricks, apparently at home. Where the gable peaks—a blue and violent sky. Everything broken, and a feeling of inexorability—which I love. Inexorability and I agree. My father, blind and desperate, but his empty eyes towards the sun. My window with a view of the valley (we're quite high up, like we were at N). Unprotected, consenting, ecstatic: *as if blood poured from my eyes.*

Should I keep a distance between myself and rational truth? N's (Socratic) attitude. Not my business.

I'll leap in. The water—swallowing you up—is *time*. Still, it's important to struggle against the tendency to *rest*. Sometimes there's no relaxation: that's when it's so attractive, and when anguish takes hold of you. If rest is easy, the danger (now remote) is just as great.

There has to be alternation.

Sometimes there has to be simulated danger—*anguish*—so that movement can be maintained. Anguish, inevitable as fear, has the advantage of eliminating relaxation, even when in principle relaxation is possible.

Anguish is there because action isn't.

Action is the effect of anguish and cancels it.

But there's more to anguish than concern for danger which requires action in reply. Anguish is fear and also a desire to be ruined (an isolate being has to lose himself and, losing himself, communicate). Anguish and the feeling of real danger mix—they're usually confused. Sometimes I'll *flee* from pure anguish through action. And sometimes there is no answering action, nothing in response to the fear that would otherwise solicit it. In that case we respond to fear as if it was anguish (especially in primitive forms: sacrifice for the sake of useful ends, when only action…).

Swimming through time's waters has its different stages:
a1) real concerns
a2) action (productive expense of energy)
a3) rest
b1) anguish
b2) partial, explosive loss of self…(unproductive expenditure, religious dementia, but categories of religion and action intermixed—eroticism is something else—laughter reaches divine innocence…)
b3) rest, etc.

Different mistakes.
All of these coming from fear of swimming, apparently.

Someone wants to go from concern or anguish to rest without acting. Someone else prefers concern or anguish, since rest disgusts him. Another's enmeshed in action that has no end. Sex impulses obsess still another. No one *realizes* what *swimming* is. Methods oppose swimming: each of them teaches you *not* to swim. Swimming: chaos, confusion itself. It wouldn't take much (consciousness, I mean) to see swimming as sickness or neurosis…. Swimming isn't a skill, it isn't learned. Swimming is a *letting-go*: *we can't desire concern or anguish*. We're so stubborn that against all evidence we're convinced (by upbringing and morality) that concern and anguish are pointless. If human enterprise indefinitely succeeded, anguish and concern would be excluded. But we couldn't be reconciled with time, since we're its negation. If success does take place, it's a veneer or facade (life of a little rich girl…).

To take account of useful action on one hand and loss on the other….

Formerly humankind would stave off its anxiety through loss (religious sacrifice), though today we try to stave off anguish with the help of useful activity. Today's attitude is more sensible (the old one being infantile). A genuinely manly attitude wouldn't allot *more*, only *more conscious*, importance to loss.

I can't justify this principle: *irreducible anguish*. In such cases, we refuse to recognize *the unjustified*, however inevitable it may be.

Lately I notice I've been switching from one anguish to another. By anguish I mean apprehension of misfortune: naked anguish evidently doesn't have an object except that we exist in time—which destroys us. The confusion is necessary. I'll make a distinction. Anguish is an effect of desire that by itself and *from within* engenders a loss of being. Fear, apprehension, and concern are so many general effects coming *from outside* dealing with needs (self-preservation, nourishment, and so on). Naturally, though, in each new apprehension it's possible that (desire's) disguised and unfathomable anguish might surface.

Threatened need is a need for more (sex-) pleasure. And in this case, anguish is nearer than it is in simpler states we share with animals—like hunger or fear of some immediate danger. An imperceptible transition from accumulation to loss is implied in this principle—that *the condition of loss is the movement of growth*, which can't be indefinite and which becomes resolved only in loss. In the simplest animal state, this is asexual reproduction.

For the individual, partial loss is a means of dying while surviving. It's foolish to try to avoid the horror of loss. At the brink of what can't be borne, desire names this horror as possible. You have to come *as close as possible* to death. Without flinching. And even, if necessary, flinching.

...and even, if necessary, dying.

Alternation of the six stages (grouped in two movements: concern, action, and relaxation / anguish, loss, and relaxation) implies a double movement: charge and discharge, potency and impotency. But while it's easy to see that action and loss exist in opposition, concern is often indistinguishable from anguish. So you have to simply say that, in alternation, you have to act *first of all* (loss presupposes action and a previous charge), *then* lose. Action without concern wouldn't be thinkable. Loss stems from unfathomable depths of anguish. There's a rhythmic awkwardness here. Laceration (which you never intend) is introduced by concern from the *outside* and by anguish from the *inside*. From inside—but in spite of conscious will, which is only a means of producing *action*.

Rereading these fragments from last year, I remember I felt death—a chill in my soul. It wasn't anguish but a chill, an exasperation with the fact of being me, an exasperation with the lack of happiness and excess I felt. But what about God? His absence was no longer bearable in my distress. The passages I reread were intended to show how this absence grabbed me by the throat—they demonstrated the *presence of God*. God lives, God loves me...that's how my feeling of fear concluded. In that moment every feeling opposing fear was annihilated—or seemed to be.

In bed this morning the first thing I thought was that God *existed*, then (going more slowly) that God, his absence and I, we were equally ridiculous—ridiculous appearances.

But without the strength of my youth (gone now!) how would I reach divinity's laughter...? Youth is excessively impulsive though! And the impetuousness of a *self* limits it.

Taking everything into account, there's a reconciliation to be hoped for with the straightforward, the young and the healthy: those opposed to complexity. No reconciliation with Christians, intellectuals, and aesthetes.

Going as far as you can: the argument about Christians, intellectuals, aesthetes disappears. It stops being important as an issue.

Always the same lack of harmony and reason. Sometimes happy, drinking, laughing. Later at the window I stop breathing. Moonlight floods the valley, outlining the terrace hedges in profile. A little later, prone on the floor, the cold tiles of the bedroom underneath me, I'm begging for death, you can hardly hear my voice.

Flowers in the woods, so lovely, this (oppressive) exhaustion of war, the different kinds of unrest, work, nourishment—all paralyzing, pushing, shoving me, cancelling me out.

The hurry and anguish come to a halt at nightfall. I go out on the terrace and lie on a deck chair. In the sky bats wheeling, darting (blindly?), emerging from the woodpile and from the bathroom, swooping down on roofs, trees, faces. Sky pure and pale now. Rolling hills stretch out into the distance, and beyond lie peaceful valleys. I'm making it a point to carefully describe this place where I picture spending the year ahead. Narrow houses, surrounded by broken-down roofs overlapping each other, the thin strip of property divided by a hedge-lined path, the terrace. High over the village walls our terrace looks out on a mass of forested hills.

After a long period of relaxation, the *absence* of starry skies triggers laughter in me.

When I'm anguished, each difficulty I encounter is insurmountable ...none when relaxed, though.

When the relaxation begins I feel diminished. I can't make love, I'm sick physically. A limp dishrag. Laughter that reaches the stars—and explosive life returns....

A first sign of anguish in me. I feel impotent, unable to introduce necessary acts into time. The harmony I have with time is broken, causing remorse—the feeling: I'm on the decline. Directly related to the fact of writing this notebook: I'm not following the plan I drew up—instead of laughing in synch with time.

There's a necessity, in this alternation, to link up with time through action. Still, action is like laughter in requiring prior relaxation (this is the mystery of movement, of the rapid linking up of movements).

I could never find what I wanted in a book, much less put it inside one. I'm afraid of looking for this in poetry. Poetry is an arrow aimed at something. If I've taken good aim, what's important (what I want) isn't the arrow—or goal—but the instant the arrow is lost, dissolved, in the night air: so even the memory of the arrow is lost.

Nothing is more embarrassing, as far as I'm concerned, than success.
With success, approbation of natural fact is implied. And with approbation there's an equivalent of God—a God who reassures and satisfies.
And really, laughter is a weird sort of success. Action and concern correspond to natural fact, but with laughter, a load of worry's off your shoulders: the frame explodes that gives order to action.

Nonetheless, to succeed is to resolve problems. I'm given existence like an enigma to resolve. Life is a test you have to pass, to win at. It's hard not to make a wonderful story of life. What I have to do is lay the mystery bare, reject its human aspects. Even if it's true that everything is a trick or a manipulation, it would be presumptuous of me to think it. Appearance is absence of motivation, and the possibility of explanation is introduced by doubting explanation's absence—that's all. Whatever else there is is complacent stupidity, giddiness, predatory—or pious—desperation.

I can't respect Jesus. Just the opposite. I can only feel complicity in my hatred for apathy or dour faces. The same desire for fluidity or intensity of body movement (which seemed impossible). And—as well?—the same innocent irony (desperate, relaxed confidence, together with a sick lucidity).

That God could arise from feelings of being miserable puts a bad light on the human condition. We can't bear distress. The feeling of God's absence is linked to disgust with beatitude.

To continue to be *self*, *my*self! My time and life in existence right now: am I the wind blowing in ripe wheat, song of the sky black with birds' wings? The bee sees me, the blind clouds....

Incomprehensible joy, inner recesses of my heart, Negro spider...poppies of the field, sun, stars, can I be something more than heaven's wildness? Then to go deep inside me again and discover endless grief, night...and death...and desire for grief, night, and death.

And what about—bitterness, WORK, dreary cities, heads bowed down, orders bellowed out (hate), the cesspool of slavishness?

I'm like some angry fly trying to get through the screen, I cling to the limits of possibility. Suddenly I'm lost—lost in a wild heaven—raised to infinite laughter. But FREE (upset with my bad attitude, my father used to say, "Work makes you free") and emancipated from slavery through CHANCE.

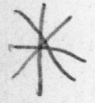

Work, though, and freedom and chance are just earthly viewpoints. The universe is FREE: it doesn't have anything to do. How could there be chance or laughter in *it*? Philosophy—extending chance beyond itself—is situated in a difference between the universe and the "worker" (humankind). Against Hegel: since Hegel tried to develop the identity of the subject/worker with his universe, his object.

Hegel, by elaborating a philosophy of work (I mean the *Knecht* or emancipated slave or worker who, in the *Phenomenology*, becomes God), cancelled out chance—and laughter.

(Laughing *in my own way*—and convulsed with laughter—I felt pain, a struggle to the death. It was dreadful and enticing. Which is *healthy*.)

If bad luck didn't exist, there wouldn't be (good) luck *in the universe* (we disclose the universe to ourselves this way). But humanness (chance) doesn't develop or become what it is without further ado. Chance discourages us, and we deify it (deny it, crucify it, nail it to necessity). Our need to *guarantee* chance, to make it eternal, is the curse of chance as flesh and blood—it's the apotheosis of a shadow we cast. We experience chance first as a rout. A reaction of fear on our part corresponds to this, and it's followed by seeking refuge in tears. Then, slowly, terribly, the tears laugh.

Parallel to the painful "metamorphosis of tears" left like sediment by swirling waters, the work of reason has continued. The God of theology exists in the interfacing of those movements.

Yesterday, an immense buzzing of bees rising up into the chestnut trees like obsessions of teenagers wanting sex. Blouses undone, afternoon laughter, the sun shines down on me with deadly laughter, rousing a wasp's stinger in me.

Each being is given a place in the world's arrangement (animal instinct and human customs), and each uses time in the appropriate mode. Not me, though—"my" time is normally a gaping wound, it gapes for me like a wound. Sometimes incapable of doing anything, sometimes rushing around—ignorant about where work begins, where it ends. Anxious, panicky, confused: unfocused. And yet, *I know better*. The anguish, though, is latent in me, and it flows out in the form of feverishness, impatience, and avarice (the stupid fear of *wasting* my time).

As I approached the summit…everything got confused. At the decisive moment there's always something else to do.

Start out…forget it…don't conclude. As far as I'm concerned that's the right method and the only one able to deal with objects that resemble *it* (resemble the world).

When? How will I die? That's of course for others to know some day. I can't know it myself. Ever.

A farmer is working his vineyard, cursing at his horse. His shouted threats raise a deadly cloud over the countryside newly awakened in springtime. His shouts attract other shouts—a net of threats darkens life. Like swearwords of laborers and farmers, and like prisons, work on assembly lines makes everything ugly. Dirty hands and lips expecting a storm....

I'm restless and don't have a job. I'm poor and keep spending my money. But if the situation's hard to put up with, it gets even more so. I live "from moment to moment"—and the moment after leaves me totally at a loss. My life is a melange—sensuality and diversion, luxury and table scraps.

I can't abide anguish which a) puts me under a strain, b) turns life into something burdensome and keeps me from really living, and c) takes away my innocence. Anguish is guilt. The movement of time needs potency and rest. Power is linked to rest. In sex, impotency derives from undue worry. Innocence, though, is an abstract idea. An absence of guilt can't be negative—it's glory. Arguably, the opposite—an absence of glory—is guilt. Guilt means being excluded from glory.

I'll go to bed, and the dreams I anticipate terrify me. I recall dreams I had other nights—ruins turning into dust. I love flowers, sunlight flooding in, the gentleness of someone's shoulder....

I'm summoning up youthful strength, energy, and the solemn or slender beauty of song. And as I age—the masculine melancholy of music.

What I used to like about nonsense and strangeness was the sparkle, the urge to dazzle, life that was lived in an easy-going, impetuous way.

The more impetuous or anxious beauty is, the more painful the laceration that results. In any case, the pain people have is co-extensive with their misery. But in glory, their pain and anguish are consumed.

With the least slippage, the movement of life is no longer tolerable. Everything is built on a foundation of slipping. The most timid laughter absorbs infinite slipping.

It's dawn as I write. As if my courage was on the verge of failing!

If it got to the point I wasn't fascinated by this or that possibility of glory, I'd be pitiful trash.

I'll overcome even petty difficulties, inability to live my life, impotence. I'm somewhat frightened by laughter, a horrible pleasure which tears you apart—a pleasure so demented I think of the knife of a murderer.

The most bitter thing for me: the misunderstanding that mars the word "glory."

But it can't be denied that human existence is linked with what this word designates. Shrugging your shoulders doesn't help. The lies of which this word's been an occasion don't alter our feeling about it. The necessary thing is getting to the core, where physical truth is disclosed.

All the earth has spoken and lived glory, and not just the glory of war. The sun is glorious, so is daylight. If something is glorious, it can't be cowardly. But this doesn't mean glory can be reduced to the glitter of disreputable undertakings. No: glory is present where life is affirmed. And chance—or people's willpower—will decide whether they affirm it in one way or another.

Glory can't be abandoned to the whims of frivolous people who divide it up like children playing with toys, using it for legal tender, selling off wild freedom to those with the money. Withdrawn from a ridiculous or sordid circulation, there remains in glory a youthful energy that consumes you and fills you with surges of pride, synchronizing you to the desires of other people.

A loyal response to the desires of others is glorious whatever else happens. But the fact that vanity can be procured from glory is a sign of its withering.

I'm teaching the most cheerful and most difficult of moralities. And this is all the truer since the difficulties in it aren't overcome with effort. Threats or the whip won't help the "sinner."

There's little hope for me. My life is exhausting … and it's not easy to maintain my childish "take" on things (a laughing playfulness). Innocence and confidence are cruel; they ignore the tension that threats produce. Given my difficulties, who could continue? Sometimes death looks preferable. I'm at the end of my rope....

I'm just as opposed to poetic mysticism as Hegel is. Aesthetics and literature (literary dishonesty) depress me. I suffer from a concern for individuality, for staging "self" (this, as it happens, is something I've indulged in). So I'm snubbing vague, idealistic, and elevated views and seeking a humdrum reality—humiliating truths.

A basic difficulty. At present, my state of lucidity (which anguish brings to the fore at the times I'm strongest) excludes relaxation, without which I'd stop being able to laugh. Action governs my present-day lucidity. Hence the impossibility of a state of loss. I could only recover my ability to laugh by rediscovering relaxation. And for now I'm not considering that.

Instead of exhausting myself in the contradictions of states of loss (through which it's disastrous to swim against the current—without willpower, in play or through chance), I'll try to show action as being in charge of those states.

3 I'm Trembling, Laughing

Can someone really *laugh to death*? (The image is bizarre, but I don't have another.)

If my life was being lost in laughter, my self-confidence would be *unknowing* confidence and so, a *total absence* of confidence. Unconstrained laughter leaves behind the areas that are accessible to speech —and starting with its conditions, such laughter is an undefinable leap. Laughter hangs suspended, it leaves you laughing in suspense. You can't keep up your laughter—keeping it up is ponderous. Laughter hangs suspended, it doesn't affirm anything, doesn't assuage anything.

Laughter is a leap from possible to impossible and from impossible to possible. But it's only a leap. To maintain this leap would be to reduce impossible to possible *or the other way around*.

To decline "maintaining" this leap—this is what happens when a movement rests or relaxes!

There's a necessity to act as soon as you no longer can either "leap" or stay in place.
My life—shattered, cut to pieces, lived in a fever, without anything to give order to it or to be a help to it from the outside—a concatenation of fears, anguish and exasperated joys—demanding a possibility, a viable means, an action that will correspond with my desires. What is required for me isn't just loving but a coming to know what means of

action can lead me to where love is possible. I have to descend to the details.

The condition of "laughter" is *knowing how* to resolve life's ordinary difficulties. Possibly the decisive thing is looking at laughter as a necessity foreign to tragedy. With a tragic attitude, the mind is overcome and is half-Christian (that is, submissive to inevitable misery); it abandons itself to the consequences of its downfall. Heroism is an attitude of escapism. The hero escapes from the misfortune he inflicts on the vanquished. Eroticism is unrelated, except in marriage, to concerns for a happy outcome. Marriage usually expels eroticism to the margins, it considers eroticism irregular, illegitimate, dangerous. Ordinary or minor laughter, like eroticism, is expelled to the margins. And, also like it, its place is only furtive.

The laughter I'm speaking of necessarily expels misfortune—it can't be furtive. It limits the horizons of—the possibilities of—humankind.

In a state of calm we can first relate to laughter, then sexual excitement and painful scenes as these come. It's incumbent upon us in a state of misfortune to love more firmly. Often misfortune will generate a heroic attitude. Or platitudes stemming from tragic feelings (Christian humility). Love associated with laughter (when everything's suspended, when we can only count on chance) isn't easy to develop and requires an extreme of tension. In this case the end of tension isn't laughter but a struggle against unfavorable conditions. (I said "love"—love of life, of possibility and impossibility, not of a woman...).

The basis of a poetic attitude is trust in natural arrangements, coincidences, and inspiration. Humanness is reducible—if it comes to that—to a struggle of nature against itself (existence when questioning itself). This struggle is given in blind arrangement (in a play of differentiated elements). Human life has a relationship to *lucidity* which isn't given from *outside* itself nor acquired from opposite conditions—a lucidity that comes from endless struggles with itself and that finally dissolves in laughter (non-knowing). Inevitably both lucidity and struggle reach an awareness of limits—wherein relative results falter and being questions itself.

In the representation of this game of being as it questions itself, the slowdown of movement would give the illusion of possible satisfaction, of flawless lucidity. Actually, so-called flawless lucidity can't be made to halt or to coincide with itself, even for one second: it destroys itself exhausting its possibility. At no time in its development is lucidity independent of questioning; and its ultimate outcome necessitates an ultimate questioning.

I'm lying down, anxiously, when the stars come out…. Getting up, I take off my clothes and my shoes, put my robe on. I go outside to the terrace, I calm down. There I am, looking at a "world" with the idea of cheerfully answering it. Proudly, madly—answering "anguishing" difficulties with the precision they required.

I wake up after midnight in a state of non-knowing, bathed in anxious sweat. I get up. Outside is raging wind, starry sky. I go to the far end of the terrace. I gulp down a glass of red wine in the kitchen. I become aware of a difficulty no specific action can respond to: if I'm subject to the consequences of a mistake. I'm assuming my mistake is stupid or my fault, though irreparable, and this is what remorse is….

There's a light shining through that resolves remorse. But the light that shines through wouldn't resolve anything if it didn't bring existence to intensity, to the point of laughter (as iron brought to incandescence).

In laughter, ecstasy is freed, is immanent. The laughter of ecstasy doesn't *laugh*, instead it opens me up infinitely. The light that shines through is traversed by laughter's arrow as it leaves mortal absence. An opening up—*deranged* as this is—implies, simultaneously, love for the arrow and a feeling of comfort deriving from an awareness of triumph.

When I laugh I celebrate defeat's marriage to power. The feeling of power is a tribute to the success of a natural element against nature— an element that questions nature. Nature would prevail nonetheless— it would elude being questioned—if the element, when it prevailed over nature, would justify nature by its success in prevailing. And that would be nature's triumph, instead of a way for nature to be questioned. To be *questioned* still means defeat. It means that *defeat is success* (that defeat succeeds), and pure lucidity cannot, in this sense, go all the way. It cannot succeed at laceration! Being, when questioned, slips into indecisiveness, turns into interference, splits apart—like laughter….

There's an indefinable gaping in laughter, something mortally wounded—this is nature, violently suspending itself.

Overcoming nature, as far as we're concerned, also means losing: because at that point we're satisfied by nature. Exhausted like the Danaïdes at a task that can't end.

Utmost lucidity isn't given in immediate lucidity, but happens when lucidity fails: the night has to fall before knowledge is possible (the humor of feverish excitement at the end of *Aminadab*, where existence is loosed from classical, that is, idealist and Christian moorings).

Questioning is a feature of isolated being. Lucidity—and a radiance that shines through—are features of isolated being.

But in the radiant shining through, in glory—this isolated being denies itself as isolated being!

When isolated being considers itself a natural existence without noting (since it's alone) the laceration in all other things and itself (the thing it is), it is by that fact in equilibrium with nature. This amounts to the repose of isolated being: struggle has come to a halt.

If I set out on the ways of questioning, my struggle against exhaustion is boundless. On such ways I struggle upstream while at each instant I'd prefer to let go and float down. All the more so because questioning endlessly obscures desired results: to possess results is to float down again. The human world seems natural because almost completely made up of erosion.

I couldn't, however, go upstream without going back downstream. *Upstream* and *downstream* are inexact. I go up when I go back down. Nature opposes nature in me. I can only question nature on the condition that I'm *it*. Areas of life that seem least natural—office work, the area of law, and tools—are, with respect to nature, relatively independent. They coexist and aren't able to bring things into question. They're separated from nature by a break in continuity (by greater comfort in satisfaction, possibly), and nature remains open to the arrangements of chance. If I desire to oppose nature, I have to lose myself in it instead of isolating myself in one of my functions (the function of being "on duty," of being an instrument).

Questioning isn't compatible with rest. A statement will be immediately destroyed as soon as it's stated. Even hurled into the possibility of movement, my written thought is unable to exhaust movement—and, being written, this thought has the immobility of stone.

I can't dwell on poetic expressions of the exhausting possibility of movement. Destroyed and scattered language corresponds with a suspended or exhausting aspect of thought; but only in poetry is it effortless or flowing. If poetry isn't committed to the experience of going beyond poetry (being distinct from it), it's not movement—it's a residue left over from excitement. To subordinate the endless excitement of bees to the necessities of harvest, to package honey, is a withdrawal from their purity of movement. Beekeeping withdraws—it withdraws honey from the bees' feverish intensity.

Further along than poetry, poets make fun of poetry; they laugh at its exaggerated sensibilities. Lust laughs at the lover's timidities in the same way. Staring at a person or kissing a person, I bring toxic passion to bear. Can this satisfy? Just kissing and staring?

God isn't humanity's limit-point, though humanity's limit-point is divine. Or put it this way—humanity is divine when experiencing limits.

I take leave of myself, destroy myself—in a certain way—and discover myself again "drowning in a glass of water."

I'm in a bad mood. My nose is longer. I don't know what to do about myself and others.

Looking at a cloudy sky cut into a proliferation of ribbons, I had an intuition about the mute tragedy of things, a tragedy even more *hounded* than Phaedra when she's dying—and the horrors of hell weigh her down....

When I read Hegel, my wounds, laughter, and "holy" lust seem misplaced, though they're only commensurate with an effort to collect scattered "humanness".

I continued along playfully, going by fits and starts, never losing sight of the beginning, excitement, or the last thing, which is night.

Often Hegel seems obvious, but this obviousness is hard to put up with.
As you go on, it's even more so. The obviousness you reach in the sleep of reason is no longer an awakening. At the end of history, with everything now obvious, humanity would change, become immutable nature. I feel threatened by death. *I*.... But in any case this kind of mel-

ancholy can't be communicated. Whether right or wrong, my feeling of "waking unto death" can only die with me. Suppose humanity continues wandering and dissipating in unending disagreement with itself.... But suppose, reaching agreement, it disappears as humanity (humanity *is* historical being and *is* lack of agreement with itself...): the mummylike afterlife of the thing written down.

The living part of the bourgeoisie is also the sick part (what's neurotic, whining, and unreal). Out in the country, a deformed population (a deaf-mute, ten years old, droning on in the bus, braying on and on —ahh, oooo, eeee, ohhhhh—and his mother with her monkey-face and big protruding lips which brush the side of his head.... A small wedding party along the way: a jolly red-faced man, pot-bellied, toad-like, was feeling up a skinny hunchbacked long-nosed woman. At the time it bothered me that I wasn't wearing clothes I liked: a bearded lady in black, closely shaved, looking out over the crowd from the height of an unspeakably immense chest). So what? I refuse to run away. I'm a human being, and there's no escape from either explosive or impotent occasions.

I can't confuse myself with the world. My own merit won't change it. The world's not me, and personally I'm nothing. The greenery that grows all around, spring flowers, unlimited diversity, and at sunset the plains and mountains and seas of the earth as it goes wheeling across skies.... But if in one sense the world is humanness (what I am through and through), that's only true provided the world *forgets* that this is what it is (a night like the end of *Aminadab* is falling).

This world, connected with vanity, wants diffused madness. It doesn't want me specifically—doesn't single me out. What the world wanted is humanness in general, meaning an unlimited dream which only makes sense at night (nonsense is the background). So it isn't me but humanness that the world wanted: an Arab, a street kid, judge, convict.

Feeling the world *wagering itself* in me, I discover exultation, there's a sense of being in sync with vanity, childishness, something to make me laugh. The fact of being sheer accident is a strength in me. I'm glad to discover within me a violence like making a smart move in a game. Blind violence....

Everything leads to one point. And in the long run the luck I might have been—the good luck—dooms me to decline. Few lives require so much effort (though appearing easy...).

Deep distress and duplicitous malice gave me a church-goer's experience of God. But this simpleminded side of myself comes from pride. Kindness, independence, and contempt for conventionality gave me the self-confidence of a gambler.

A feeling for gambling—being the Don Juan of the possible—is the source of the comic part of my nature (and the origin of infinite laughter in me).

Man isn't born to resolve the problems of the universe but in fact to discover where the problem commences and then to maintain himself within the limits of the knowable.
Goethe, *Conversations with Eckermann*

But our humanness is suspended from an enigma that constitutes us, and our unsolvable nature is the source of glory, delight, laughter, and tears.

Goethe concluded that "human reason and divine reason are two quite different things." Goethe presumably was taking on the establishment position, namely, Hegel.

Hegel's attempts appear unhealthy, even ugly, when compared to Goethe's serene balance. Hegel at the summit of knowledge doesn't have this cheerfulness. "Natural consciousness," he says, "immediately hands itself over to science"—the word represents a system of absolute knowledge—"and this is another attempt on the part of consciousness to walk on its head. It does this unaware of what causes it to do so. When natural consciousness is constrained to move this way, a violence is imposed on it which appears without necessity and for which nothing has prepared it." (*Phenomenology*, Preface) How full of life Goethe seems, innocently disposing of the resources of the world, instead of the other's constrained and slightly ludicrous position. Still, I'm only free and easy, relaxed (more playfully, I'm only *Goethean*) when *beyond* Hegelian misery.

Goethe adds, a bit further on, "We shouldn't utter dicta of the highest worth unless they can be used for the good of the world. As for the other dicta—we have to keep them to ourselves since they'll always be there diffusing their light like a concealed sun on everything we do." Isn't it odd that real wealth acts blind and that divinity tends to impotence? Hegel's constrained position versus the mortuary beauty of Goethe. Only "infinite laughter" enlightens me.

Without Hegel, I'd first have had to be Hegel—and I lack the means. To me nothing's more alien than personal modes of thought. To hate individual thought (a spoiled brat insisting "That's not what *I* think ...") is a way of reaching calmness and simplicity. If I utter a word, I bring into play the thought of *other people*. This is a thought, it so happens, I've gleaned from the human substance surrounding me.

One lovely day in spring: you get up and wash, you shave, you brush your clothes off.... Each morning there you are, a new man, scrubbed clean, shaven, clothes brushed.

Just as the accumulated grime of day has to be washed off, I overcome the darkness of chance (difficulties of thinking).
What I call night is different from the darkness of thought—night has the violence of light.

Night itself is youth and drunken thought: it's youth and drunken thought to the extent it's night, to the extent that it's violent discord. If humanness is discordancy in terms of itself, in its vernal drunkenness it's night. Its gentlest springtimes stand out against a background of night. Night can't be loved by hating the day—nor day by fearing night. The Greek dancer, drunk with beauty, shame and youth, dances with a figure that is death. The marvels of the dance come from each dancer loving the other dancer's denial of him (or her) and their love reaches the very limits where the seam of time bursts asunder. Their laughter is laughter itself.... Each makes use of and in turn is used by the other. If this night was purer, it would be the certainty of day; and day would be the certainty of night. Tension arising from suspension is necessary to the discord from which accord comes; and refusing to remain what it is, accord becomes even more an accord, harmony becomes more harmonious.

4 Will / Willpower

Deep truths. An afternoon in the country, a warm sun beating down in May. In my room behind closed shutters, I'm hot, happy, and my jacket's off now. An expansive wine making me feel a bit tipsy, but I've got to go down and use the *rest* room....

The two movements in eroticism. One's in harmony with nature; the other questions it. We can't do away with either. Horror and attraction intermingle. Innocence and the explosion both serve play. At the right time, doesn't even the silliest woman know what the dialectic is?

What I write is different from a diary in this way: I have a mental picture of someone not too young, not too old, not too subtle, but not too practical, pissing and crapping unself-consciously (cheerfully). I picture him (after reading me) considering eroticism, reflecting on a questioning of nature. He'd then see what pains I take to lead him to a *decision*. Why analyze this? Let him think of the times he's been innocently (darkly, unmentionably) aroused—he's questioning nature.

Eroticism is the brink of the abyss. I'm leaning out over deranged horror (at this point my eyes roll back in my head). The abyss is the foundation of the possible.

We're brought to the edge of the same abyss by uncontrolled laughter or ecstasy. From this comes a "questioning" of everything possible.
This is the stage of rupture, of letting go of things, of looking forward to death.

As with war's more unpleasant moments, the arbitrary is expelled from the ways I follow. Imagination is unbearable if it doesn't reach out towards specific objects. I'm struck by the organization in my writing —it's so strict that after an interval of several years the pickaxe hits the same spot. (There's almost no loss when I compare what I wrote then to what I'm writing now.) A *system* precise as clockwork governs my thoughts (but I escape endlessly in this incompletable work).

I'd belong to a somewhat changed species of humanity, one that has to overcome itself. This species would combine action and questioning (work and laughter).

Knowledge opposes the final doubt of questioning to the sureness of action. But life makes each a condition of the other. Submission to nature (to confusion seen as providential) is an obstacle to *action*. In the same sense, action itself is a struggle with nature. On the other hand, impotence in realizing action (poetic laziness) leads directly—or as an after-effect—to the recourse to divine authority (submission to the natural order). The divine freedom of laughter intends nature to submit to humanness and not the other way around.

I was looking at a photo taken in 1922. In it I'm on the roof garden of a house in Madrid; it's a group photo. I'm sitting on the ground with my back to someone. I recall feeling playful, even chic. The way I lived then was foolish. In time, the reality of the world—of the universe—refracts like a ray of sunlight in a prism, and time flings it in all directions. Hills, swamps, dust, other human beings are just as united, just as indistinct as particles of a liquid. A horse, a fly!—All mixed up.

absence of thunder
pouring waters stretching out to eternity
and I'm happy as a fly
or a hand someone has cut off
and I'm the one who drenched these sheets
I was the past
blind a dead star

yellow dog
there it is now
horror
screaming like an egg
puking my heart out

handless
I'm screaming

I scream to the sky that it's
not me! it's not me screaming
in this lacerating thunderstorm
it's not me dying
it's the starry heavens
starry heavens drenching me
while I fall asleep
and the world is forgotten

bury me in the sun
bury every girlfriend I've had
bury my wife and her nakedness
in the sun
bury the kisses I've given
and the white drool on my mouth

A man drums his fingers on the table for an hour, then gets red in the face. Another has two boys dead of TB, and his daughter, who's crazy, is strangling her two children, etc. A strong wind springs up…and everything (taking us along), raging, sweeps us to meaninglessness. Dreams of other planets arise out of weariness. I'll be frank and say that the idea of escape isn't crazy or shameful. We want to find what we're searching for—and that is to be freed of ourselves. That's why there is such a feeling of intoxication when we find love, and when it's missing why there's such huge despair. When love is another planet, we collapse in it, free of the emptiness of our strumming and unhappiness. In fact, in love we stop being ourselves.

This, against the reader's drowsy indifference. He puts the book down a moment later. And for what? Does he have an appointment with himself?
This, against the "in my opinions," against intentional differences.

I use language in a classical way. Language is an organ of will (action comes from it), and expressing myself is a function of the will, which continues on this path till the end. What would it mean to speak of relinquishing will in an act of speech if not—romanticism, lies, unconsciousness, and poetic messiness?

To me the most radical, valid thing is to bring intentional movements into opposition with the innocence of ecstatic laceration. Ecstasy can't be an intentional goal for us, still less a means working towards some other result. Lack of concern with the paths leading to ecstasy can't exclude the fact that ecstasy assumed these paths. Still, speaking, sinking into your own words, necessarily involves you in looking for those paths—dawdling over willed impulses, you're not able to challenge the means to which you agree your life is reduced.

I see a necessity for acting with *unplanned* boldness, dryness, and lucidity. I have a naked feeling about how heavy reality is. Horror won't stop making me sick, but it's my wish to love this weight *unreservedly*. Existence has to go to extremes, it has to accept real limits and these limits only—or would laughter be possible? If I obligingly dwelt on disgust, if I denied a weight I couldn't raise, I'd be "liberal" or a Christian—and in that case how could I possibly laugh?

The horizon in front of me (open horizon). Beyond it are villages, cities with human beings eating, speaking, sweating, undressing and going to bed. As if they didn't exist. The same thing with the people in the past. The same with those in the future. But to this world beyond the hill and beyond the moment, I'd like to give the clarity of phrases like "But to this world beyond the hill…" and so on. What I am can't reach Stendhal now that he's dead. And who will ever do more for me than I'm doing for this dead man? In the beyond of the hill and of the moment I'll die like a spent wave…. Meantime, in my bed I've dozed off. I wake up. Sky pale on the horizon, setting sun streaking it. A lovely golden star, a delightful crescent that I glimpse through light clouds, beyond hills and beyond the moment…. Sleep! I shake it off and I write, hoisting myself up to the pinnacle of this writing like a flag, so I can see (and be seen) better. Then in a little bit comes the sleep again, exhausting as breathing my last.

Is it possible for me to escape a state of fatigue, my gradual collapse into death? And what trials and tribulations there are in writing a book, in the struggle against the exhaustion of sleep, in the desire for the clarity of a book—a gleam slipping from cloud to cloud, from landscape to landscape, from one sleep to another! I don't have a hold on what I'm saying—sleep is starting to overcome me. What I'm saying is decomposing into a death-like inertia.

One sentence slipped a little further into the decomposition of things and I was already asleep…I forgot it. I wake up afterwards, writing out these few words. Already things are falling…a rubble of sleep cascading down….

If I could just be a field in the morning fog. And I picture a crow cawing in it.

I write like a bird singing as dawn approaches. With (unfortunately!) anguish and nausea bearing down—terrified by dreams of night. I tell myself over and over, "Someday I'll be dead—DEAD!" What about the magnificence of this universe *then*?! It will be nothing. All my senses X'd out, new ones take shape, as elusive as waterfalls. A wind's blowing harshly in my head. To write is to take one's leave, to go someplace else. The bird that sings, the human being who writes—are delivered. Again, sleep. And, head nodding, I let go.

And now that night's over, where will I be going? My strength in not caring, my happiness in not knowing…where I'm going.

I laugh infinitely about this, and as long as I live I want to laugh. Laughter takes on life's intensity, its passionate willpower.

I make love the way some people weep, and laughter alone is proud; only laughter intoxicates with the sureness of triumph. Letting yourself go, not acting from your own will (but from God's or nature's), you won't find it in you to laugh, you won't experience laughter's infinity.

Laughter's like feet: normally ruined when shoes are worn.

I'm not writing for *this* world (surviving, intentionally, the world that war has emerged from). I write for a different world—one that's indifferent to anything, anybody. I haven't any wish to impose myself on it and think of being there quietly as if absent. Clarity implies recognizing the necessity of having to disappear. I'm in no way opposed to real strengths or necessary connections: only idealism (hypocrisy and lies) makes a virtue of condemning the real world and ignoring the *physical truth* of it.

What am I if not a ray from some long-dead star? The world whose light *is* me is dead. It's hard to have to do away with the difference between this real death and the imitation which is my life.

From a decomposing, dying, or dead world, what still remains in the form of light is the negation of that world (of its truth, of its order). It's not an expression of the world to come. Is it a message from one world to another? Or a dying old man who leaves behind him a sign of life? After I die who will experience the vanity of this life of mine? And who then will let loose the animal cry of a life filled with every possibility, dying in the flames of excessive potentiality?

I'm reading Stendhal's *Journal* for March 30, 1806:

Madam Filip is stretched out on a daybed in her yellow drawing room, the key to which her indolent daughter finally found. She belches, and I'm thoroughly disgusted with her. A voluptuous face and sighs—especially inhaling medicinal vapors. That way lies death!...

Before this, Samadet made a fool of himself in the eyes of only twenty people, like Pacé and me. English duets, voices that won't stay on key. This poor society, so desperate for excitement! You have to be very careful not to bore them with the pointlessness of things. Just don't be obscure, though that is what you are if you give any indication of wit. Tuf de Wildermeth seen for what he is—this very day.

This man made a study of being dignified. The right face, the right height, a touch of cruelty, a lean and elegant expression, all conspire to make him quite the acceptable fellow. If this character were his choice, you would have to assume he is wittier than he is. Stiff too, and lacking good taste and gracefulness, but a Lovelace from Marseilles—and feelings are his means of seduction.

"This man...." Samadet? Wildermeth?
At the bottom of a shaft: Samadet sings in society.
The other side of the coin, a horse tied to the wall along a street in A. The rope invalidated its huge head—a non-existent misfortune. The horse should have run away. It was like the wall or the ground.

How can you deny your own head (relinquish autonomy)? Wildermeth is a horse himself, a piece of meat, a fragment (takes himself for more). Pride can't be localized, but it is. Often I'm human, I rebel. Then a little later? I'm a horse or Samadet.

I forget nothing. I'm speaking to Samadet: only foolishness (only Samadet) reads me, a horse doesn't. Conceit and foolishness, what the earth denies as it turns. Since you're my reader, Samadet, I'm your gravedigger! And you never lived!

Every evening, a star at the same place in the sky. I'm relative to the star. Possibly this star's unchanging and, looking at it, it's possible I'm not (me, anyone, no one). The ridiculousness of a flea or housefly's ego is dispelled in the ridiculousness of a star.

Only a star....
Any star, whatever. Whatever it is that makes a star a star.... Humanity *is* when it knows it isn't. Matter *is* insofar as it dissolves man and, in decay, reveals an absence.

An opaque *I* sustains the universe in its opacity....
It would be futile to try to take precautions against this. Christian humility is disastrous, above all contradictory, related to an inevitable obsession with a *self!* Think of the monstrous immortality of the *egos* that are heaven and hell! Think of the God of *self* and the demented way he has ordered self's replication!

I'd like from now on to see the *self* in relation to something else. Man, or *self*, is actually related to nature, and therefore is related to what he denies.
Relating to what I deny I am, I can only laugh at this, be dispersed, dissolve.

Laughter doesn't deny just nature (in which we're entangled) but human misery (in which most of us are still entangled).

Idealism (or Christianity) relates humankind to that in man which denies nature (to idea). Nature being conquered, humanity in dominating it has the power of relating to what it dominates—it has the power of laughter.

Pride is the same thing as humility: always a lie (Wildermeth or St. Benoît Labre). Laughter, pride's contrary, is sometimes a contrary of humility (no one laughs in the Gospels).

I can only worship or laugh (I get the upper hand through innocence).

5 The King of the Wood

I've had so much to say. My testimonial? Incoherent! I was the light that moved when the clouds did, gathering and coming apart. Weakness itself. Cowardice, fatigue, and boredom with life undid me, and I was released from human customs (to which death bound me!).

A personal need to act in order to take possession of life's possibilities demoralizes me. What binds me is my need for pleasure.

I'm weak. I'm anguished. Not a moment passes when my legs don't give way from *vertigo*. Suddenly my pain pierces heaven, it's a pain that assumes *insanity....* (There's strength in me to laugh in response.)

There's no refuge on earth or in heaven for me.

That is God's only meaning, the claim to being my refuge. But can a refuge be compared to a lack of one?

The idea of God, affection, acts of sweetness associated with him—these are preparations for God's absence. In the *night* of this absence, these insipid delights and signs of affection have disappeared, reduced to the inconsistency of childish memory. The element of terrifying grandeur in God heralds an *absence* in which we are stripped bare.

At the summit man is staggered. He is, at the summit, God himself. He's absence and sleep.

The dialectic of *self* and totality is resolved in me through exasperation. When negation of *self* is seen as obliged to merge with totality, it is the basis of that dialectic. But in particular, this movement wants questioning itself to replace the person being questioned; it wants questioning to replace God. When the questioned totality becomes questioning and only questioning, what is questioned stops having a name to define it. Questioning remains a fact of isolate being, but what is questioned in the first place is that isolate being itself.

The dialectic is stymied right at the outset this way. By questioning or speaking, a questioner or speaker is quashed. But if he sinks down, deep down, into this silence, this absence, down to its depths, he becomes the *prophet* of what's lost there.... He is contemptuous of God and of individual human beings, whose presence is manifested in sentences. At one and the same time, he's an enthusiastic joker and someone who feels contempt for such jokers. The majority of those who speak and, as they speak, never stop saying *I*, emanate from such a questioner! They emanate from his silence!

But I can't X myself out.... And this book amounts to a naive assertion of myself. To be honest, I'm only the laughter that takes hold of me. The impasse I sink into and into which I disappeared is only the immensity of the laughter....

. . . .
. . . .
. . . .

I'm the king of the wood, Zeus, a criminal....

. . . .
. . . .
. . . .

My desire? It doesn't have limits....
Did I have it within me to be the same as *Everything*? I did...ridiculously....
I made a leap. I leapt to the side.
Everything disintegrated, dispersed.
Everything in *me* disintegrated.
Could I for an instant *not* laugh?

(Just a man like any other.
Fussing about his obligations.
Repudiated in the clear wishes of the majority.
Laughter is a bolt of lightning in this man as it is in others.)

In the depths of the woods, as in a bedroom where two lovers are undressing, laughter and poetry are set free.
Outside the woods, just as outside the bedroom, useful activity goes

on; each person is a part of it. But inside the bedroom, each person withdraws from useful action: and when we die, each of us withdraws from the possibility of action.... In the woods my craziness rules as sovereign.... Who could suppress death? I'm setting fire to a golden bough; flames of laughter can be heard within, licking at it.

The obsession with speaking has taken up its home in me, an obsession with exactness. I see myself as a precise, capable, ambitious person. I should have kept quiet but I'm speaking. I react to the fear of death with laughter—it stimulates me!—while I struggle against it (against fear, against death).

I write. I don't want to die.
To me, the words "I'll be dead" can't be breathed. My absence is a wind from outside. It's an occasion of laughter—my pain is an occasion of laughter. In my room, I'm protected. But the grave? It's so near already, the thought of it shrouds me from head to toe.

There are such contradictions in my attitude!
My frank sincerity is like a dead man's. Has anyone ever been so serenely, happily frank and sincere?
But ink changes absence into intention.

Did a wind from outside write this book? To write is to articulate an intention.... I intended this philosophy *"whose head was near heaven while its feet adjoined the realm of the dead."* I'm waiting for the onslaught of a squall to uproot.... Right now I'm in touch with everything possible! At the same time I'm in touch with the impossible. I'm attaining the power of existence to reach the opposite of existence. My death and I slip away together into the wind from outside where I open myself *to my absence.*

There's a shelter near the summit of a mountain (Etna) that I recall reaching after an exhausting walk, which included two or three hours of night walking. Above the 2,000 meter mark nothing more grew—there was dusty black lava. At 3,000 meters, it was horribly cold (freezing) at the height of a Sicilian summer. A raging wind. The shelter was a long hut used as an observatory, and on top of it a small dome had been added. Before falling asleep I stepped outside to answer a call of nature. I felt a chill right away. The observatory separated me from the volcano's crest, and I walked along the wall under a starry sky looking for the right spot. The night was relatively dark and I was intoxicated with weariness and cold. Coming from around the corner of the shelter, which till then protected me, a huge, fierce wind took hold of me with a thunderous roar, and I was offered the chilling sight of the crater two hundred meters above. The night didn't prevent me from taking in the extent of the horror. I stepped back, frightened, protecting myself, then—gathering my courage—stepped forward again. The wind was so cold, the roar so deafening, and the volcano's summit so fraught with terror I could hardly bear it. Today it seems to me that never had I been made to gasp for air with such force by the *non-me* of nature (the climb up, difficult anyway, even if I'd wanted to make it for some time—and I had come to Sicily for just this reason—exceeded the limits of my strength, and I was sick). I couldn't laugh from my exhaustion. All the same, climbing along with me, from the beginning, was infinite laughter.

A nagging wish (I want to keep expressing myself to the bitter end): but finally I'm indifferent and I laugh.

You get what you want in a sneeze. I express an absence of concern as will. I saw I was supposed to *do* this or that—and I'm doing it (my time is no longer this gaping wound).

1943

APPENDIX

(Letter to Blank, Instructor of a Class on Hegel...)*

Paris, December 6, 1937

Dear Blank,

Your complaints against me help me express myself with greater clarity.

I admit—as a likely assumption—that as of now, history's finished (except for the wrap-up).† All the same, my ideas on things are different from yours....

It doesn't matter. The experiences I've lived through and been so concerned about have led me to think there is nothing more for me "to do." (I wasn't inclined to accept this and, as you saw, didn't go along with it until I had to.)

If action ("doing") is (as Hegel says) negativity, then there is still the problem of knowing whether the negativity of someone who "doesn't have anything more to do" disappears or remains in a state of "unemployed negativity." As for me, I can only decide in one way, since I am exactly this "unemployed negativity" (I couldn't define myself with more clarity). I admit Hegel foresaw this possibility, but at least he didn't situate it as the outcome of the process he described. I think of my life—or better yet, its abortive condition, the open wound that my life is—as itself constituting a refutation of Hegel's closed system.

---

* The draft of this letter was described as destroyed (or lost) in "Misfortunes of the Present Time"; it was added to the fragments of a work I started, then published in this appendix. This incomplete letter wasn't copied out, although the draft was given to the addressee.
† Maybe mistakenly. Mistakenly at any rate in what concerns the twenty years that followed. Blank thought the solution—revolutionary Communism—was at hand.

The issue you raise with regard to me comes down to knowing whether I'm insignificant or not. Obsessed with a negative answer, I've often raised this issue. In addition, as the idea I have of myself varies, and as it happens sometimes that I forget (comparing my life with lives of more noteworthy people) that it could be mediocre, I've often thought that at the summit of existence there could be only insignificance. In fact no one could "recognize" a summit that would be night. Several facts (like the extraordinary difficulty I experience in getting "recognized" at the simple level at which others are "recognized") led me to take the hypothesis of "irrevocable insignificance" seriously, but cheerfully.

This doesn't bother me, and I'm not linking the hypothesis to any possible pride. But I wouldn't be human if I accepted it before trying to avoid a plunge into the depths (by accepting it, I'd probably become still more comically insignificant, bitter and vindictive—and in that case I'd have to rediscover my negativity).

What I'm saying about this hypothesis invites you to think a disaster is coming, and that's all. In your presence, I have only an animal's justification of itself, squealing because its foot is caught in a trap.

Truly, disaster and life aren't the issue any more. What we're talking about is this—what will "unemployed negativity" *become*, if it's true it becomes *something*? I keep track of it in the forms it creates, not first in myself but in others. Most often, powerless negativity becomes the artwork—though it's with difficulty that this metamorphosis, whose consequences are usually genuine, corresponds to a situation created by the end of history (or by the thought of its ending). An artwork answers evasively or (inasmuch as its answer is prolonged) it doesn't correspond with a particular situation; it's extremely ineffective as an answer to the final situation when evasion is no longer possible (when *the moment of truth* arrives). In what pertains to me, the negativity that is mine gave up being employed only when it couldn't any longer be employed: it's the negativity of a man who has nothing more to do, not of a man who prefers speaking. But the (undeniable) fact that negativity excluding action is expressed as artwork isn't thereby less laden with the meaning of action, insofar as possibilities existing for me are concerned. That fact indicates that negativity can be objectivized. Moreover, such a fact doesn't belong to art as its exclusive property, since religion makes negativity an object of contemplation better than a tragedy or a painting. But negativity isn't recognized *as such* in the artwork or in the emotional elements of religion. Just the opposite: it's introduced into a system that nullifies it, and only the affirmation is recognized. Thus there is a fundamental difference between the objectivization of negativity in the form the past has known and the one that remains possible *at the end*. In fact, when the man of "unemployed negativity" doesn't find in the art work an answer to the question he himself is, he can only become the man of "*recognized* negativity." He has grasped that his need to act is no longer employable. But since this need can't be deluded indefinitely by the deceptions of art, at one point or another it will be recognized for what it is: negativity without content. Still, the temptation presents itself to reject this negativity as sin. This is such a convenient solution that humankind didn't wait for a final crisis to adopt it. Since this solution has already occurred, its effects have been exhausted beforehand. The man of "unemployed negativity" almost can't dispose of its effects anymore. To the extent that he's a consequence of what preceded him, the feeling of sin loses its grip on him. He confronts his own negativity as if it's a wall. However uneasy he feels about this, he knows that after this nothing can be ruled out, since negativity has no more outlet.

(Fragment on Knowledge, on the Fact of Action, and on Questioning)

On one hand I'm contemplating the givens of practical knowledge, and on the other, man's questioning of everything that is, of nature and of himself (we oppose nature and question it, but we couldn't realize this opposition without opposing ourselves and without at the same time being a questioning of ourselves).

The facts of practical knowledge are the basis for answers that defer this questioning and postpone it to some point further along, to a later date. In fact we first question in limited forms, though this questioning has itself unlimited content. We look for the origin of this or that, its reason for being, its explanation, but we lose sight of the fact that our results (with respect to the desire involved in speculative knowledge) have the same meaning as steps on the stairs that lead to night.... Actually, disinterested knowledge, philosophy, and the dialectic summarization of them are facts testifying to an *overlap* between practical knowledge (certainty tied to the *fact of action*) and *infinite questioning*. But in spite of this hybrid nature (between meaning and loss of meaning), the development of knowledge beyond crude results isn't simply an empty exercise. Even from the standpoint of practicality, dialectical knowledge is applicable in at least one definite area. How does this double development have a meaning? In other words, how and under what conditions can a movement of questioning, to which there's no end, enrich practical knowledge?

A priori, the effectiveness of struggle won't be any surprise. The exhausting nature of metaphysical questioning can't be eliminated in any way, but unsuccessful efforts at the level of questioning (since these efforts have no purpose except themselves) can eventuate in a level of activity and crude knowledge; that is, their authenticity is proved by being put into action.

CRUDE PRACTICAL KNOWLEDGE, SCIENTIFIC
KNOWLEDGE, AND THE DIALECTIC

The initial certainty is the certainty of work, of the tool, of the man-made object, and a regular relationship of work to the object: rudimentary knowledge is know-how. My knowledge of an object I've made is a full and satisfying knowledge to which I try to relate the knowledge I have of other objects—natural objects, myself, and the universe. But the propositions that come from know-how are *logical* statements. Beginning with crude certainty, language sets up a series of equivalent situations. For the criterion of know-how it substitutes that of mathematical rigor, which is at first only an enrichment of this know-how. On one hand this substitution extends technical possibilities in the most useful way; on the other, through a shifting, it introduces certainty to a place beyond the possibilities of action (in the realm of speculation). But soon certainty, thus developing inside language, takes on a dialectical look. First of all, formal and rigorous certainty is opposed to immediate certainty. It borrows the feeling of conviction, the confidence of "I can" from the original; but it challenges its exterior nature. This first operation already develops the possibilities of a dialectic: at the same time that language states positive propositions, it opens up a wound in us by means of interrogation. What translates the opposition of two certainties is already a questioning of certainty, and every questioning bears within it an infinite interrogation to which there's no conceivable answer and in which the absence of an answer is obscurely *desired*.

If I'm deceived about a crude notion—thus, about my belief concerning the hardness of a piece of wood, expressive of solid consistency and undoubted material reality—I say this for the benefit of a learned representation of the same object. But whatever the case, the new representation is implicated in a dialectic of infinite questioning. Once having challenged my naive certainty about the wood, my new certainty, having a questioning as its foundation, keeps itself in movement. At each stage the certainty of "I can" is found in a new form—and every mode of representation of the real is founded on the fact of action, on possible experience.

Thus science itself has a dialectical nature insofar as its foundation is a questioning.

PHILOSOPHY

All the same, science only proceeds as an outer questioning. Challenging the sensible qualities to which immediate certainty was tied, science contents itself with substituting quantities for them. And when it leaves the realm where exact measure is possible, it has recourse to the equivalence of connections. But it never seeks to understand objects fundamentally. It's true, science can't extend its mode of exterior comprehension to totality—totality doesn't allow itself to be reduced to explanation through equality and can only come arbitrarily within the province of knowledge that has *know-how* as its basis. This powerlessness (or impotence) leaves the way open for infinite questioning and (with good reason) is held as equally insignificant. However, powerlessness is minimized by the fact that science looks with distaste on problems it can't resolve. Thus as far as science is concerned, questioning never gets beyond the restlessness required for activity.

However, philosophy takes on a strange dignity from the fact that it supposes infinite questioning. It's not that results gain philosophy some glamour, but only that it responds to the human desire that asks for a questioning of all that is. No one doubts that philosophy is often pointless, an unpleasant way of employing minor talents. But whatever the legitimate biases on this subject, however erroneous (contemptible, even heinous) the "results," its abolition runs into this difficulty—that exactly this lack of real results is its greatness. Its whole value is in the absence of rest that it fosters.

(Two Fragments on the Opposition of Humanity and Nature)

I

It isn't as a definite thing that humanity runs into conflict with nature (and it's likewise not as a definite thing that nature is against humanity).

Humanity's is the effort to be autonomous.

In one sense or another this effort takes place according to contingent situations.

In principle nature appears as confused: human existence is what is tempted to remove itself from the confusion, to reduce itself to the purity of rational principles.

And the domination of nature by human beings is assured in this movement; nature is brought into action by those who subject it and make it serve their autonomy.

But in every situation (every situation is provisional) human existence relies on a *middle term*. Humanity can't claim autonomy in its own name. The brain's clarity of thought (our capacity to make judgments) allows us to note the vanity of the movement that constitutes us. For when we grasp ourselves as a movement towards autonomy, we perceive our confusion and the deep dependence in which a confused nature holds us. Hence the necessity to relate to ideal middle terms, such as "God" or "reason."

God or reason are middle terms in this sense—that each is related to confusion of some kind and to a graspable order inside the confusion.

God is related to tangible signs, to the interpretation of confused nature, as if nature were clothed with negative meaning: Christian nature is at once a temptation (what you have to overcome) and an order (what you have to submit to) concealed under tempting appearances. Christianity *arranges* elements of this given confusion in the midst of which we seek our autonomy, and so separates good from evil.

In this separation, the will to autonomy in the human head is regarded as evil. The head only realizes its autonomy—to which it's nonetheless dedicated—indirectly. The head is subordinated to God, whose image it is—who's neither nature nor some negation of nature, but the director of good in nature's confusion.

As the one who directs good, God is already reason. But he's creative reason, which guarantees and explains nature—and not only the order in it, but its whole confusion. This confusion isn't evil. Evil is the fact that in the confusion some creature wishes to possess an autonomy that belongs only to God!

The nature that humanity (in a Christian situation) denies is a paradoxical aspect of nature. It is essentially human nature. And this nature, being a will to autonomy in nature, is basically the negation of nature!

In itself this situation is inconceivable. It's coupled with the truth of another, cruder situation. Christianity has strengthened and developed man's negation of his animal nature. Man is defined, in essence, as a rejection of two positions.

1) Nature = human nature, will to personal power. Autonomy = God, the one who directs nature, which is wholly in harmony with him except in one point: where nature is a negating of nature in the species of humankind;

2) Nature = animal (or carnal) nature: which in humankind doesn't tend towards the will to autonomy, and so, sensuality.
Autonomy = intellectual and moral tendencies.

In position 1, God, reduced by mankind to a negation of man, is forced into a general assertion of nature in which the key part, autonomy, is lost (essentially autonomy is negation or intolerance). In this position man abdicates, and the autonomy which he enters in God is only a deception. He's no more than an infant in the arms of a fool.

Thus position 2 is necessary not just for man but for God. To be honest, Christianity is based on this involvement of mankind's intolerance towards nature, to which we submit as animals—but this movement turns towards the inhibition of the will to autonomy.

The two positions rest on misleading assumptions.

In the second, opposition to nature is the opposition of an existence which would *like* to be and isn't. This sort of autonomy, to which the human mind aspires, isn't its own autonomy but that of a purely speculative existence (set up as a mode of attributing being to words) and pure intellectuality and morality. The challenge to nature has to be made by a real being, a being who is able to assume that challenge itself; it isn't made by some hypostasized desire or pure morality which necessary human behavior expresses. Already, in this simple position, the condition of autonomy is defined as inaccessible.

God is only an attempt to attribute being to a condition of autonomy (which appeared inaccessible to man). But insofar as he is God, insofar as he asserts nature…the initial movement falls into slavery to nature (the theological developments that are directed in a contrary sense—God transcending nature—underscore an impossibility, his impossibility, of denying nature and defying it: the most that can be said is that if God transcends nature, he can't *question* it. That *by all rights* can't become his night).

Recourse to reason represents a renunciation on the part of humanity. Replacing the puerile game of the believer, who speaks to God like a child to its doll, there develops a behavior of the same order (founded on the attribution of being to words) though less naive, more noble and susceptible of being exceeded.

In pure recourse to reason, the situation's hardly changed. Man renounces—by opposing it to animal confusion—a principle in which he participates (necessarily with some difficulty). And this principle is scarcely less than God's involvement in nature; he's the *director* of nature. If one pays attention to things insofar as they're given historically, this principle is drawn out of confusion as a negative. Reason is language opposing general forms and common measures to things, or at least to a confused nature (since this confusion is immediately given in things); it is language opposing logical order to chance. But reason, as God, reduces man to a hybrid position. On one hand, man condemns his own greediness for autonomy (*contrary to reason*). On the other, he continues to oppose the "animal" tendencies in him, which he denigrates insofar as they don't tend towards his own autonomy, and insofar as they sink him into the confusion of nature. In this way he only exchanges one type of sinking for another; reason, which seems autonomous to him, is itself only a natural given. It's in no way autonomy but a renunciation of this premature Christian renunciation, implemented through a loathing of animality.

Clearly, in the two cases (God and Reason) this type of breakthrough into unreality is a result of the substitution of language for the immediacies of life. Man has doubled real things—and himself—with words that evoke them and signify them and outlive the disappearance of the things signified. Put into play in this way, these words themselves make up an ordered realm, adding, to precisely translated reality, pure evocations of unreal qualities, unreal beings. This realm replaces being insofar as immediate being is sensible consciousness. For the formless consciousness of things and oneself there is substituted reflective thought, in which consciousness has replaced things with words. But at the same time that consciousness was enriched, words—calling to mind both unreal and real beings—took the place of the sensible world.

So it is that as regards God, and then reason, the autonomy sought by man for himself is readily constituted (in several ways) in a realm of unreality to which human life is related.

But because of *the fact itself* of this unreality, the development of language as thought (as a form of being) is necessarily dialectic. Language propositions are produced in a contradictory manner: their fixity distances itself from the real, and only their contradictory development has any chance of relating them to it. Only a "dialectic" has any power to subordinate language—or the realm of the unreal—to the reality it calls to mind.

This couldn't be realized from the outset as a renunciation of "logos." What Hegel said about reality was that it is "logos," even when envisaged in the totality of its (contradictory) development. According to Hegel, reason isn't unreal abstraction; a human being of flesh and blood is reason incarnate. Hegel was the first to resolve a demand for autonomy in a human sense. In Hegel's eyes, man's mind is absolute being. Nature itself realizes autonomy of being, but in a negative development. Being as it develops effectuates the negation of nature, or rather the development of being is the same thing as this negation. Reason is effectively realized in the negation of its contrary. Nature is the real obstacle necessary to the effective reality of the negation: this is the condition of "logos." The rationality of dialectical reason inversely reflects the irrationality of nature. Without nature and the effort that dialectical reason had to make to extricate itself from it, dialectical reason wouldn't have been realized effectively, would only exist as a possibility.

The fact is, whether it's God who's in question or pure reason or Hegelian reason, there is always "logos" substituted for man seeking autonomy. The identification of Hegelian reason with man is precarious and equivocal. Crudely, what distinguishes man from nature, what *opposes* man to nature, is history—and completed history. Man integrated into nature would cease to be distinguished from it. Now according to Hegel, the identity of man and reason assumes that history is finished: nothing meaningful, from that time on, would *take place* on earth. All developments pointed to a stage when man wouldn't be distinct from reason anymore—they were only stages towards a point! That point having been reached, no development is possible; infinitely, as with animal nature, man will be identical to himself, and every possibility of *historical* event will be bypassed.

Of this view of the mind I retain the basics: in searching out autonomy (independence with regard to nature), man is led—by language—to situate this autonomy in a (logical and unreal) middle term, but if he gives reality to this unreality—becoming it himself (incarnating it)—the middle term he utilizes becomes in its turn nature itself.... Unless the whole development is only a mental view....

As soon as man places the autonomy he desires in some middle term, that middle term, whatever it is, takes the place of nature. But the consequences of autonomy thus appear only in a purely negative fashion.

Only the presence of authenticity—positive difference—gives meaning to the critical attitude.

Human autonomy is linked with *a questioning of nature*, a questioning and not the answers to this. The previously stated principle has to be taken up again under a more general form: every "answer" to the "questioning" of nature takes on the same meaning for man as nature does. That means: 1) that essentially man is a "questioning" of nature; 2) that nature itself is the essential—the basic given—in every response to a questioning. The ambiguity of these statements comes from the fact that nature is in one sense a defined area, but that in a deeper sense this area is properly the in-depth response suggested by the questioning of man (suggesting itself as a springboard to infinite questioning). In other words, every "response" to fundamental questioning is a tautology: if I question the given, in my answer I can't go further than a new definition...of the given as such. Questioned, for a time the given ceases to be such; but if I've answered, whatever the answer, it'll become the given.

No "answer" can offer man a possibility of autonomy. An "answer" subordinates human existence. The autonomy—sovereignty—of man is linked to the fact of his being a question with no answer.

2

If to the question "What is there?" human existence answers in any other way than "Myself and night, that is, infinite questioning," it makes itself subordinate to the answer, that is, to nature. In other words, man is explained from the fact of nature and thereby renounces autonomy. The explanation of human existence that starts with the given (any roll of the dice substituted for any other) is inevitable but empty insofar as it *answers* infinite questioning: to formulate this emptiness is at the same time to *realize* the autonomous power of infinite questioning.

(Fragment on Christianity)

Basically Christianity is only a crystallization of language. The solemn assertion of the fourth Gospel—*Et verbum caro factum est*—is in a sense this deep truth: the truth of language is Christian. If you assume man and language as doubling the real world with another world, imagined and available when evoked—then Christianity is necessary. Or if not, then some analogous assertion.

(Fragment on Guilt)

I'm appealing to the friendship of human existence for itself—for what we are (at the moment) and what we'll be, for the fate that's ours, that we've willed, our loathing of natural givens, and goals outside us to which we submit in weariness (love or friendship implies this loathing).

Every "response" is an outside order, a morality inscribing human existence in nature (as a creature). Submission makes man into a non-man, a natural being, but broken and humbled by *himself*, so as to no longer be the insubordination *he is* (in which asceticism is a *humanness* that remains in him and is insubordination reversing itself, turned back on itself).

Belief in poetry's (or inspiration's) omnipotence is upheld in Christianity, but the Christian world cheats at its madness, and what it calls inspiration is essentially a language of reason.

Human existence is guilty: it *is* this to the degree it opposes nature. A humility that makes humanity ask forgiveness (Christianity) overwhelms human existence without excusing it. Christianity's advantage is that it at least aggravates the guilt it proclaims....

The only way to reach innocence is to be rooted firmly in crime: man questions nature *physically*—in the dialectic of laughter, love, ecstasy (this last envisaged as a physical state).

In our time everything is simplified: mind no longer plays the part of opposition, it's finally no more than a servant, the servant of nature. And everything takes place at the same level. I can excuse laughter, love, and ecstasy...though laughter, love, and ecstasy...are sins against mind. They physically lacerate *physis* or nature, which mind sanctified as it incriminated mankind. Mind was the fear of nature. The autonomy of a man is physical.

Negativity is action, and action consists in taking possession of things.

There is taking possession through work;
    work is human activity in general,
    intellectual,
    political, or
    economic;
to which is opposed
    sacrifice,
    laughter,
    poetry,
    ecstasy, etc....,
which break closed systems as they *take* possession.

Negativity is this double movement of "action" and "questioning."
Likewise, guilt is associated with this double movement.
Human existence *is* this double movement.

The freedom of the double movement is linked to absence of response.
Between each movement and the other, interaction is necessary and incessant.
Questioning develops action.
What's called mind, philosophy, and religion* is founded on interferences.
Guilt arises in a zone of interference—on the way to an attempted accord with nature (human existence is guilty, it asks forgiveness).
The feeling of guilt is a *renunciation* by man (or rather, his attempt at renunciation) of a double movement (of negation of nature). Each interference is a middle term between man and nature—and a *response* to the mystery is both a brake on this double movement (a gentle and in fact *reactionary* interference) and a (practical) system of life founded on guilt.
Humanly speaking, stopping the interference is a lie (it's a response, it's guilt, it's the exploitation of guilt).

* Religion in this sentence doesn't have the meaning of religion independent of given religions but of whatever religion is given, among other religions. [1960 Note]

Intellectual "givens" have meaning on the level of being action, and they respond to being questioned (they proceed from this) to the degree that interaction is possible, which is to say exclusively on the level of being action.

Still, an infinite questioning (pruning away mediocrity and interference) accords with an ultimate and systematic action (human existence defines itself as a negation of nature and renounces its guilty attitude). Hence a sort of non-religious sacrifice, laughter, poetry and ecstasy, partly released from forms of social truth.

Action and questioning are endlessly opposed. On the one hand as acquisition for the benefit of a closed system, and on the other, as a rupturing and disequilibrium of the system.

I can imagine an action so well conceived that the questioning of the system for whose benefit it took place would now be meaningless; in this case, precisely, the questioning could only be infinite. However, the limited system could still be questioned again: criticism would then bear on the absence of limits and the possibilities of *infinite* growth in acquisition. In a general way, insofar as questioning is laughter, poetry…it goes hand in hand with expenditure or a consumption of surplus energy. Now, the amount of energy produced (acquired) is always greater than the amount necessary for production (acquisition). Questioning introduces a general critical aspect that bears on the results of a successful action from a point of view no longer that of production, but its own (that of expenditure, sacrifice, celebration). Action from then on is likely to shore up any response at all, to escape questioning that challenges its possibilities of growth. In this case, it would be brought back to the confused level of interference—to the category of *guilty*. (Everything continually gets mixed up with everything else. Would I still be this implacable theoretician, if a *guilty* attitude didn't remain in me?)

What I propose isn't an equivalent of a *response*. The truth of my assertions is linked to my activity.

As assertion, the recognition of negativity only has meaning through its implications at the practical level (it's linked to my attitudes). My continual activity is linked first of all to ordinary activity. I live, I fulfill the usual functions that found great truths in us. And from there the opposite aspect commences: the method of questioning prolongs the establishing of original truths in me. I slip from the trap of responses and take the critical viewpoint of philosophies to its logical conclusion—as clearly as I distinguish objects among themselves. But bringing negative thought to action isn't limited to prolongations of general activity; on the other hand, this thought realizes its essence when it modifies life. It tends to undo ties—detaching the subject from the object brought into action. Moreover, this sort of activity, intimate and intense, possesses a field of development of basic importance. Beginning with intellectual operations, what's at issue is an infrequent, strange experience which is difficult to bring up here (but which isn't less decisive for that). But this—ecstatic—experience doesn't essentially have the nature of a monstrous exception which would first of all define it. Not only is it easy of access (a fact that religious traditions don't mind keeping hidden), but it obviously has the same nature as other common experiences. What distinguishes ecstasy is, rather, its relatively developed (at least in comparison with other forms) intellectual nature, *susceptible* in any case of infinite development. Sacrifice, laughter, eroticism, on the contrary, are naive forms that exclude clear awareness or receive it from the outside. Poetry, it's true, surrounds itself with various intellectual ambitions—sometimes even intentionally sows confusion between its procedures and "mystical" exercises—but its nature returns it to naïveté (an *intellectual* poet is made restless by interference, by a submissive, *guilty* attitude to the point of logomachy. But poetry remains blind and deaf. Poetry is poetry, in spite of the majority of poets).

Neither poetry nor laughter nor ecstasy is a response; but the field of possibilities that belongs to them defines activity linked to assertions of negative thought. In this realm, the activity linked to questioning is no longer exterior to it (as it is with partial challenges, which are necessary to the progress of science and technology). Negative action is decided freely as such (consciously or not). However, in this positioning, agreement with pure practical activity is an accommodation with the fact of the abolition of interference. Thus man comes to the point of recognizing *what he was*. (It can't be said in advance, though, that he won't find his greatest danger in this fashion.) Maybe an agreement with self is a sort of death. What I've said would be annihilated as pure negativity. The very fact of success would remove the opposition, dissolve man in nature. Once history's finished, the existence of man would enter animal night. Nothing is more uncertain than this. But wouldn't the night need only this as its initial condition—that we remain unaware that it's night? Night that knows it's night wouldn't be night but would be the fall of day...(the human odyssey ending up like *Aminadab*).

(Two Fragments on Laughter)

I

We have to distinguish:
—Communication linking up *two* beings (laughter of a child to its mother, tickling, etc.)
—Communication, through death, with our beyond (essentially in sacrifice)—not with nothingness, still less with a supernatural being, but with an indefinite reality (which I sometimes call *the impossible*, that is: what can't be grasped (*begreift*) in any way, what we can't reach without dissolving ourselves, what's slavishly called God). If we need to we can define this reality (provisionally associating it with a finite element) at a higher (higher than the individual on the scale of composition of beings) social level as the sacred, God or created reality. Or else it can remain in an undefined state (in ordinary laughter, infinite laughter, or ecstasy in which the divine form melts like sugar in water).

This reality goes beyond (humanly definable) nature insofar as it's undefined, not insofar as it has supernatural determination.
Autonomy (with respect to nature), which is inaccessible in a finished state, functions when we renounce that state (without which it's not *conceivable*); that is, in the abolition of someone who wills it for himself or herself. It can't therefore be a state but a *moment* (a moment of infinite laughter or ecstasy...). The abolition takes place—provisionally—at a time of lightning-like communication.

CORRELATION OF RUPTURE IN LAUGHTER
WITH COMMUNICATION AND KNOWLEDGE
(IN LAUGHTER, SACRIFICIAL ANGUISH,
EROTIC PLEASURE, POETRY AND ECSTASY)

In laughter, in particular, there is a knowledge given of a common object (which varies according to the individuals in question, the times, and races, but the differences aren't in degree, only in nature). This object is always known, but normally from the outside. A difficult analysis is required if an inner knowledge of it is attempted.

Given a relatively isolated system, perceived as an isolated system, and given that a circumstance occurs that makes me perceive it as linked with another (definable or non-definable) whole, this change makes me laugh under two conditions: 1) that it's sudden; 2) that no inhibition is involved.

I recognize a passer-by as a friend of mine....

Someone falls to the ground like a bag: he's isolated from the system of things by falling....

Perceiving its mother (or any other person), a child suddenly undergoes a contagion—it understands that *she* is like *it*, so that the child moves from a system outside it to one that is personal.

The laughter of tickling comes from the preceding, but it's the sharp *contact*—a rupture of a personal system (insofar as it's isolated within)—that's the underscored element.

In any kind of *joking*, a system that's given as isolate liquefies, falls suddenly into another.

Deterioration in the strict sense isn't necessary. But if the fall is accelerated, say, this works in the direction of suddenness; while the factor of the situation of the child, the suddenness of the change (the fall of the adult system—that of grown-ups—into an infantile one) is always found in laughter. Laughter is reducible, in general, to the laugh of recognition in the child—which the following line from Vergil calls to mind: *incipe, parve puer, risu cognoscere matrem.** All of a sudden, *what controlled the child falls into its field*. This isn't an authorization but a fusion. It's not a question of welcoming the triumph of man over deteriorated forms, but of intimacy communicated thoughout. Essentially, the laugh comes from *communication*.

---

* In a meeting of the College of Sociology, Roger Caillois, citing this line on the subject of laughter, remained reticent about the meaning. It is possible to translate "Begin, young child, to recognize your mother by your laughter" also as "by *her* laughter." [1960 Note]

Conversely, intimate communication doesn't utilize exterior forms of language but sly glimmerings analogous to laughter (erotic raptures, sacrificial anguish, or—in poetry—evocation). The strict communication of language has as its object a concern for things (our relations with things), and the portion which it exteriorizes is exterior beforehand (unless language becomes perverse, comical, poetic, erotic…or unless it's accompanied by contagious procedures). Full communication resembles flames—the electrical discharge of lightning. Its attraction is the *rupturing* it is built on and which increases its intensity in proportion to its depth. The rupture which is *tickling* can appear to the will in an unattractive light—laceration and discomfort are more or less sharply felt according to the forms. In sacrifice, rupture is violent, and often violent in eroticism as well. You find it again in the laugh Vergil refers to: a mother provokes a child's laughter by making faces at it, leading to the disequilibrium of sensations. She brings her face suddenly near her child, engages in games of startling expressions or makes funny, little cries.

The main thing is the moment of violent contact, when life slips from one person to another in a feeling of magical subversion. You encounter this same feeling in tears. On another level, to look at each other and laugh can be a type of erotic relation (in this case, rupture has been produced by the development of intimacy in lovemaking). In a general way, what comes into play in physical or psychological eroticism is the same feeling of "magical subversion" associated with one person slipping into another.

In the various forms whose foundation is the union of two beings, rupture can enter only at the beginning, and the contact afterwards remains set: then the intensity is less great. *Intensity of the contact* (and thereby the magical feeling) *is a function of resistance*. Sometimes removing an obstacle is felt as a delicious contact. From this there results a fundamental aspect—these contacts are *heterogeneous*. What fusion brings into me is *another* existence (it brings this *other* into me as *mine* but at the same time as *other*); and insofar as it's a transition (the contrary of a state) and in order to be actually produced, fusion requires heterogeneity. When the transition factor isn't involved (if the fusion's accomplished, it's only a state), only stagnant water subsists, instead of the waters of two torrents mixing together with a roar; the removal of resistance has changed fusion into inertia. Hence this principle: the comic (or erotic) elements are exhausted in the long run. At the moment the waters mix, the slipping of this into that is violent. Resistance (the same that an individual sets up in opposition to death) is violated. But two similar individuals can't endlessly laugh or make love in the same way.

Laughter, though, only infrequently corresponds to the outline of compenetration. Ordinarily what it puts into play is a comic object, facing which it's (theoretically) sufficient to have one person laughing, not two. As a general rule, two or several people laugh. The laugh reverberates, amplified from one person to another, but those laughing may be unaware—they may be—of their compenetration; they can treat it as a negligible element or have no awareness of it. It's not among those who laugh that the rupture takes place and otherness comes into the picture, but in the movement of the comic object.

The transition from two people laughing to several (or one person) brings into the interior of the realm of laughter the difference that generally separates the realm of eroticism from that of sacrifice.

The erotic struggle can *also* (in drama) be given as spectacle, and the immolation of a victim can *also* become a middle term between the believer and his or her god: lovemaking isn't less tied to compenetration (of two beings) than sacrifice is to *spectacle. Spectacle* and *compenetration* are two rudimentary forms. Their relationship is given in the formula: *contagion* (the intimate compenetration of two beings) is *contagious* (susceptible of indefinite reverberation). The development of the two forms in the interior of the realm of laughter contributes to its inextricable nature. It's easy to discern their articulation in another way: in the difference between love and sacrifice and in the fact that each can have the value of the other (lovemaking's interest as spectacle and the element of intimate compenetration in sacrifice).

If there's *contagious contagion*, it's because the element of spectacle is of the same nature as its reverberation. The spectacle is *for others* what the compenetration brought into play is for *the two individuals*. In the spectacle, and more generally in each theme brought *to the attention of others* (in puns, anecdotes, etc.), the compenetrating elements don't seek out their own interest. But those who suggest these themes pursue the interest of *others*. It's even unnecessary for two individuals to be involved. Most frequently compenetration (contagion) sets two worlds against each other and limits itself to a transition, to the fall of an individual of *one* of these worlds into the *other*. The most meaningful fall is death.

This movement is related to an intermediate figure, in which compenetration again involves two individuals; one of them, the one we look at (*the actor*), can die. It's the death of one of the terms that gives communication its human character. From that time on, it no longer unites one individual being to another, but an individual being to the beyond of beings.

In the laughter of tickling, the one who's tickled goes from a tranquil state to a convulsive state—it alienates him, he undergoes it and it reduces him to the impersonal state of living substance; he escapes from himself and so opens up to another (who tickles him). The one who's tickled is the spectacle the one who tickles watches, but they communicate; the separation of spectacle from spectator isn't effectuated between them (the spectator is still an actor, isn't a "viewer," etc.).

I'm bringing up the following supposition: that a tickled person, being intoxicated—just for fun and as a joke—might kill his tormentor. Not only does death inhibit the laughter, but it abolishes any possibility of communicating between the two. This rupture of communication isn't only negative: it is, from another view, analogous to ticklings. The dead person had been united with the tickled person through the repeated rupturings of tickling. Similarly murder unites the tickled person with death—or rather, since the dead person is dead, with the beyond of the dead person. On the other hand, from the very fact of death, the tickler is separated from the tickled person like the spectacle from the spectator.

Alleluia
The Catechism of Dianus

You must know in the first place that everything with a manifest face also has a secret one. Your face is noble: the truth in its eyes comprehends the world. But the hairy parts under your dress have as much truth as your mouth. These parts secretly open on filth. Without them, and without the shame associated with using them, the truth your eyes command would be stingy and ungiving.

Your eyes open up on stars and your hairy parts on.... This vast globe on which you crouch bristles at night with dark and high mountains. High, high above snowy peaks, the starry clarity of heaven is suspended. But from one peak to another, abysses gape and sometimes echoes of falling rock can be heard. In the brightness at the base of these chasms is the southern sky whose brilliance corresponds with the dark of the northern one. In the same way, one day the sinks of human iniquity will be the sign of lightning pleasure for you.

It's time your delirium learns the opposite of each thing you know about. Time to take the boring, depressing image of the world in you and turn it upside down. If only I could see you already lost in abysses where going from horror to horror you'll reach truth! A noxious stream pours from the sweetest cavity of your body. You avoid yourself when you distance yourself from those unmentionable outflowings. If instead you follow along in this depressing wake, your nakedness, released now, will open to pleasures of the flesh.

·

Peace and relaxation are impossible for you now. This world from which you come and which you are gives itself only to your vices. Unless your heart's deeply corrupted you'll be like the mountain climber who falls asleep forever only steps from the top—you'd be only an exhausted heaviness, only a fatigue. What you have to know secondly is: the only pleasure worth desiring is the desire for pleasure and not the pleasure. The journey your youth and beauty take you on is no more different from notions of pleasure-seekers than from those of priests. What would the life of a pleasure-seeker be, if not one that's open to whatever happens, open first of all to the emptiness of desire? In a way that's truer than the moral ascetic, the slut who's hot for it learns the emptiness of every pleasure. Or rather the taste of disgust in her mouth gets her hotter, and this leads to even more disgust.

Not that you have to refrain from canny searching. The emptiness of pleasure is a core of things which, if perceived at the outset, would never be reached. It's the delights of immediate appearance that you must learn to yield to and give yourself up to.

·

Now I have to explain to you that the difficulty I raised in point two shouldn't be considered discouraging. Insufficiency of wisdom in former times, or rather people's moral destitution, led them to avoid what seemed vain to them. Today the weakness of such conduct can easily be seen. Once we set our feet on the paths of desire, everything's empty, everything's deceitful, and God himself is an exasperating emptiness. Yet desire remains in us as a challenge to the very world that infinitely conceals its *object* from that desire. Desire's like laughter in us—we stop caring about the *world* once our clothes are off and we abandon ourselves immoderately to the desire for desire.

Such is the inexplicable fate we've been doomed to by our refusal to accept fate (fate's unacceptable nature). We can only throw ourselves into a pursuit of signs related to emptiness at the same time as maintaining desire. We're alive only at the top of the crest, a flag flying high as the ship goes down. With the slightest relaxation, the banality of pleasure or boredom would supervene. We can breathe only at the extreme limit of a world in which bodies open—in which the nakedness we desire is obscene.

To put it another way: our sole possibility is impossibility. You come into the power of desire by spreading your legs, showing off your unclean parts. If you couldn't feel the position was forbidden, desire in you would soon die, and with it the possibility of pleasure.

·

If you stopped looking for pleasure and abandoned—as too manifestly deceptive—the assumption that pleasure can be a solution to suffering or *a way out* of it, desire would stop leaving you naked. You'd succumb to an attitude of moral caution. You'd be a shadow of your former self, you'd stop playing the game. To the degree you're taken in by the idea of pleasure, you yield to the ardor of your desire. It's high time you realize how necessary cruelty is. Without decisive boldness (never justified) you wouldn't put up with the bitterness you feel when intensely craving pleasure, as soon as that craving victimizes you. Your common sense would tell you to concede defeat. Only impulses towards holiness or dementia in you can sustain the burning darkness of a desire that exceeds even the furtive gleams of orgy.

This maze is the outcome of a game where mistakes are inevitable and have to be endlessly repeated, and in it nothing is more necessary to you than to be as innocent as a child. Of course, there's not a *reason* for you to be innocent, and there's hardly a reason for you to be happy. You'll have to have the boldness of perseverance, though. It's clear that the enormous effort asked of you by circumstances will exhaust you, although there's not time for you to be exhausted. By falling into depression you'd waste yourself. A special type of cheer, one you can't make up or pretend to—a cheer like the angels of heaven—will be asked of you when you're in the anguished throes of pleasure.

One of the hard trials in store for those who are stopped by nothing relates to the necessity in them to express inexpressible horror. When they can only laugh at horror—having come to and experienced it only to laugh at or, better, to get off on it. It also won't come as a surprise if, just when you reach the other side, disaster seems to overtake you. This is generally the ambiguity of all things human. As the inevitability of horror becomes more and more unqualified, you'll be led that much swifter into joy. Everything in me dissolves, and I explode in a rage to live—a rage that's adequately expressed only in despair. Without childish naïveté, could you support this inability to take hold of things, this inexorable necessity not to circumscribe...?

.

In this sense my hopes in you go as much beyond canny resolution as despair or emptiness. Childishness has to proceed from a lucid intellect, a childishness that forgets its source (an impulsiveness with the power of annihilating). Isn't the whole secret of life the innocent destruction of whatever threatens to destroy enjoyment of life? The plain and simple triumph of childhood over obstacles hindering desire—the course of untrammeled pleasure, a secret of dark corners where you, little girl, have been known to lift your skirt....

2

If your heart begins to beat faster, think back on those childhood days of obscenity.

With the child, several moments exist but they're separate—
  ingenuousness
  pleasure-filled play
  filthiness.

An adult ties these together, attaining in filthiness an ingenuous pleasure.

Filthiness with no infantile shame, play without childish pleasure, and ingenuousness without the desperate impulses of childhood—they're all pretenses that adults are compelled to, reduced to by seriousness. Holiness, on the other hand, maintains the ardor that fuels childhood. The worst impotence is a seriousness succeeding at being serious.

Naked breasts and obscene sex organs are able to bring about what you, when you were a little girl, only dreamed of in your inability to actually *do*.

3

Weighed down by icy melancholy, by life's majestic horrors! I'm at the end of my rope! Today I'm at the edge of a pit. At the edge of the worst eventuality, of unbearable happiness. But at the top of these giddy heights, I'm singing an *alleluia*—the purest and most painful you'll ever hear.

Tragic solitude's a halo, a garment of tears to cover your slut nakedness.

Listen to me. I'm speaking in your ear and talking quietly. Stop misunderstanding my gentleness. Go naked into the night of anguish until you come to a side path.

Between your fingers, inside damp convolutions. The delight you'll have feeling pleasure's harshness in you, its stickiness, the damp stale smell of contented flesh. A mouth that in its anguish is eager to open contracts in pleasure. In loins that the winds have stripped bare twice, you'll feel a crackling gristle roll back your eyes in their sockets.

In the solitude of a forest, at a distance from the clothes you've thrown down, you'll gently crouch—a she-wolf.

A feral stink of lightning and a lashing storm, these are obscenity's companions in anguish.

Rise and flee—childish, crazed, laughing out of fear.

4

The time has come to be hard. I have no option but to turn into stone. To live during times of misfortune and be threatened…. Unshaken, confronting terrifying eventualities and for this to drop into my own depths, to be stone—is there a better way to answer the excesses of desire?

Surfeits of pleasure, kindling the heart, laying waste to it, obliging it to be hard. A holocaust of desire giving my heart its infinite boldness!

By coming sexually till you can't any more or by drinking to unconsciousness you subvert life's timidities and hesitancies.

Passion is no friend of weakness. Asceticism is rest compared to the feverish ways of flesh.

Now imagine the whole world opening up to disaster, imagine you have no conceivable protection. What's to be expected is hunger, cold, fury, captivity, dying uncared for…. Think of suffering, despair, and destitution. Do you assume you won't be their victim? Before you lie blasted wastelands—will you find help screaming out? Keep in mind from now on you'll be a bitch attacked by ravening wolves. This bed of misery is your native land, your only true home.

In any case furies with snakes for hair will accompany you in pleasure. They'll hold your hand and be faithful companions—gorge you with strong drink.

The convent's silence, asceticism, peace of mind are recommended for those you can't admire, obsessed with thoughts of shelter. For you, on the other hand, protection can't be imagined. Alcohol and desire will expose you to the raging assaults of the cold.

The convent removes you from the game, but there'll come a day when sister burns to spread her legs.

Is pursuing pleasure something cowardly? Yes, it's a desire for satisfaction. Desire, on the other hand, is avid not to be satisfied.

The specter of desire necessarily lies. What's presented as desirable is masked. Sooner or later the mask falls. Then anguish is unmasked, as is the annihilation of perishable existence. Truly, truly, you long for the night. But you have to take the indirect way; your way is to love friendly faces. These desirable faces proclaim the possession of pleasure, which quickly becomes possession of death. But death can't be possessed—it's dispossession. Which is why the scene of pleasure disappoints. To be disappointed is life's bottom line, its core truth. Without experiencing exhaustion and disappointment you wouldn't ever know—at the precise moment your courage fails—that insatiable craving for sex is death's dispossession.

To go looking for pleasure is far from cowardice, it's life's remotest edge, a raving courage. It's a ploy used by a horror in us of ever being satisfied.

Naturally, love's the most distant possibility. Again and again obstacles conceal love from the mania of love.

Desire and love are confused with each other. Love's a desire to possess an object as great as the totality of desire.

Love's insanity becomes sane when moving towards more insane love.

.

Love makes this demand. Either its object escapes you or you escape it. If love didn't run away from you, you'd run away from love.

Lovers discover each other only in mutual laceration. Each of the two craves suffering. Desire desires in them what's impossible. Otherwise desire would be quenched, desire would die.

When lack of satisfaction begins to prevail, you should satisfy your desire. You should lose yourself in the bosom of unutterable happiness. At that point happiness is the condition for increasing your desire, and satisfaction becomes desire's fountain of youth.

5

Stop being blind to *who you are*. Could I desire you humiliated, obliged to approach others with a face not your own?

You could always decide to be respectable, to enjoy the esteem of the servile. It would be easy to gauge the angles from which you'd aspire to measureless falsification. Knowing you were lying wouldn't mean much. You'd answer the servility of the majority with your own servility, robbing existence of passion. In that condition you'd be Mrs. Whoever. I'd hear them singing your praises....

You had to choose between two ways. You could have been approved of by members of a humanity founded on disgust of humanity, you could have been considered one of them.... Or you could open yourself up in freedom of desire beyond the limits of convention.

In the first case, you would have been defeated by exhaustion....

But how could I forget about your power of involving existence itself? Consider the immoderate passion exciting you *under gray skies*.... How long could you go on hiding it under your dress? Could you continue repressing wild cries and searing pleasure (which others reduce to lukewarm phrases demanded by convention)? Would you be less fascinating than night's nakedness when you're covered with shame?

Only the unbearable pleasure of lifting your dress is equal to the vastness...of knowing you're lost. Can vastness wear a dress, any more than you? And losing itself in it, your nakedness has the simplicity of dead people. In it, your nakedness is a vast display. Nerves all on edge, wracked by shame—a *you* immensely involved in obscenity.

(Isn't it to the silent, naked intimacy of the universe that you open yourself with giddiness? Doesn't an always unfinished universe yawn between your legs? What answers are there to these questions? If you took off your dress, opened yourself to the stars' infinite laughter, could you still doubt that the distant emptiness at that very moment would be lighter than the unspeakable intimacy concealed inside you?)

Sprawled out, head thrown back, eyes lost in a celestial milky flow, let the stars have...the sweet outpourings of your body!

Breathe in the sulfurous smell, inhale the Milky Way's odor of naked breasts: the purity of your loins will open to dreams falling in unimagined space.

Sex organs copulating, naked caterpillars, some bald, others like pink caves, the clamorous din, the dead eyes: continual spasms of mad laughter, aspects of you that correspond to the sky's unfathomable cleft....

Your fingers glide into a rift that hides night. The night falls in your heart. Shooting stars streak the night where your nakedness is open like the sky.

What flows out of you in pleasure (in a sweet distaste of flesh) others steal from death's immensity.... They steal it from the solitude of sky! It's for this you'll have to flee, hide in the depths of the forest. What lacerates you and gives you pleasure evokes giddy loneliness—pleasure requires feverishness! Only the whites of your eyes can recognize the blasphemy that links your voluptuous wound to the emptiness of a star-studded sky.

Who could measure up to your unbridled passions? Only night's silent immensity, vastness.

When love denies limited existences, it gives them in return an infinity of emptiness. It limits them to waiting for *what they are not.*

6

In the ordeal of loving, I escape myself. Naked, I reach the unreality shining through.

Not to suffer any more, not to love, limits me, on the contrary, to ponderousness.

A love that's chosen opposes lust. As love purifies, the pleasures of the flesh become stale. A child's nasty curiosity is replaced by transport, by innocence full of traps.

Judging from simple asexual cells, a cell reproduces because it isn't able to maintain the integrity of an open system. So that the minuscule being's growth results in overfullness, excess in laceration and loss of unity.

Reproduction of sexual or gendered animals and human beings can be divided into two phases, each having these same aspects—overfullness, excessive laceration, and loss. Two individuals communicate in the first phase through the channel of their lacerations. A more violent communication doesn't exist. In each person, the hidden laceration (like the imperfection or shame of existence) is laid bare (expresses itself) avidly adhering to the laceration of the other person. When lovers meet, it's a delirious situation of mutual laceration.

.

The fate of finite beings leaves them at the edge of themselves. And this edge is torn. (Hence the meaning of *curiosity* as tearing.)

Only cowardice and exhaustion keep you on the sidelines.

Leaning over the precipice, you intuit horror in the depths.

From every direction other torn bodies approach. Sick like you from the same horror. Sick with the same attraction, too.

Under your dress the slit's hairy. In the emptiness, opening on a confusion of the senses, a play of lights exhausts you with pleasure and makes you tremble.

Endlessly beyond ourselves in absence, the desperate emptiness of pleasure would choke us—unless hope existed. In a way hope deceives, but how would it be possible to feel the attraction of the void if the appearance of the opposite wasn't also there?

In the throes of pleasure, emptiness isn't yet really emptiness, but *a thing*, which is to say symbol of nothingness—filth. Filth produces emptiness insofar as it (filth) is disgusting. Emptiness is disclosed as disgust which attraction can't overcome. Or overcomes with difficulty.

Truth, the bottom line of despair and licentiousness, is their filthy, disgusting look.

.

Death's image, muck, proposes disgusting emptiness to being. The filth around death mimes emptiness. I flee it with desperate energy. But it's not just my energy fleeing, it's also fear and trembling.

Nothingness, *which isn't*, can't dispense with a sign....

Without which nothingness (since it isn't being) couldn't attract us.

From the moment fear and nausea are produced (in this way causing desire), disgust and fear become the apex of erotic life. Fear pushes us to collapse. But the sign of emptiness—filth—doesn't just have the power to summon collapse. It has to be linked with attractive appearances, has to compromise with collapse, so that we're held in a continuing alternation between nausea and desire. The sex organs, linked to filth, are an outlet for this, but they only become an object of desire when their nakedness is filled with wonder.

.

Young, beautiful...your laughter and voice, your glamour seduce a man. But his sole desire is this: to wait for the moment when pleasure in you mimes death, taking him over the edge, crazed.

Lovely and an offering, a silence, presentiment of unfathomable skies, your nakedness can be compared to the horror of nighttime, whose infinity it points to. This is what can't be defined and what raises to our faces the mirror of infinite death.

Expect a lover's sufferings to annihilate him. It's impossible for us to be more than a power within ourselves to open up emptiness, self-destruction. This means: stormy passions, revolt, malevolent obstinacy, obstinacy that's also cynical, affectionate, playful, and pushes you right to the brink of nausea.

This game, a play of attraction and fear—in which emptiness as it pulls the ground away abandons you to a thrill of joy in which lovely appearance, by way of contrast, takes on the meaning of horror—is by nature a thing to link up the contraries it convenes. Two beings of flesh and blood, clothed at first and then naked (each doomed to serve as a mirage to the other, then to destroy this mirage and reveal anguish, filth, and death), are undone by a game that plays them, abandoning them to the impossible. Your love is your truth if you've been abandoned by it to anguish. And in you desire has desired only to fail. But if it's true the person with you is truly a conveyor of death, if the power of attraction exercised by that person allows you to go into the night for a moment, then you must surrender unconditionally to the childish passion *to live*. From now the only dresses you'll have will be torn dresses, and your filthy nakedness will consign you to the ordeal of wild cries.

Two individuals mutually choose each other. Their goal, following strongest attractions: sexual disaster. In them alone can possibility wholly come into play. The strength needed is greater, since beauty, strength, courage are signs of failure. But the virtue of courage is shallow; it's incumbent on you to collapse into a horror of being.

Desire leads from beauty's emptiness to fullness. Perfect beauty, with its alert, imperious, and irrefutable movements, has the power to kindle laceration and likewise bind, delay it. Laceration gives beauty its deadly halo. Under favorable conditions it links purity of form to the possibility of infinite uneasiness.

Two lovers give themselves by convening nakedness. Thus they lacerate each other and remain tied to these lacerations for some time.

Beauty is from the other world. It's empty, it's a pulling out and up, something plentitude lacks.

Nothingness: the beyond of limited being.

Strictly speaking, nothingness is what limited being *isn't*. You could say it's an absence, an absence of limit. Taken from another point of view: nothingness is what limited being desires, desire having for its object *something that isn't doing the desiring*.

In love's first impulse, love yearns for death. But yearning for death is itself an impulse to go beyond death. Going beyond death, yearning aims at the "beyond" of individuated being. This is revealed by the fusion of lovers, who confuse their love with the love each has for the other's sex. Thus love associated with choice slips endlessly towards an impulse of nameless debauchery.

Isolate being dies in debauchery. Or, for a while, gives way to the horrible indifference of the dead.

In an individual slipping towards the horrors of debauchery, love attains its intimate meaning at the brink of nausea. But the opposite movement (an instant of reversal) can be more violent. At that moment the particular chosen being discovers himself or herself again, but he or she loses the intelligible appearance linked with definite limits. In any case, from the fact of being chosen, the object of your choice is fragility—the ungraspable itself. Coming into contact with the unknowable was itself unlikely, and too, it's unlikely the object of choice will be maintained. So the object is suspended above the nothingness it isn't, causing desire to be intolerable for you. But this object isn't just a minute atom consigned beforehand to an immense void; precisely the thing that causes it to be an accomplice to what destroys it is its excess life, its strength. Its irreplaceable individuality is a finger that points to the abyss, to the immensity of such an abyss. It is itself a provocative disclosure of the lie it is.... Individuality is the revelation of a woman who shows her lover her *obscene* parts. A finger designating laceration. It's the identifying mark of laceration, you could say.

To those who avidly desire laceration, individuality is necessary. Laceration wouldn't be *itself* if not a laceration of a particular person, a person chosen for his or her plentitude. Excess life, fullness, are a means of highlighting the void, and this fullness and this excess are *that person's* to the extent that they dissolve us, taking away the safety rail that separates us from the void. Hence this deep paradox: it's not simple laceration that intensely lacerates us, but rich individuality, absurd and delirious, abandoning us to anguish.

The individuality of the chosen person is the apex; at the same time it's the decline of desire. The fact of reaching the summit implies a descending. Sometimes, on its own, individuality voids itself of meaning, it slips into regular possession, is slowly reduced to insignificance.

7

Beyond the rush linked to lost obscenity you'll reach a stage of the rule of friendship. You'll again be helpless at this stage, which is more fraught to the extent a long twisting lightning bolt hangs suspended over you—consciousness of distress equal to yours. In this consciousness what completes nakedness is this certainty—that the lightning makes nakedness desirable. Shared grief is a joy this way, but sweet only assuming it's shared. The fact of both parties being lowered together into the pleasures of nakedness alters this state, and the nakedness of each of the lovers is then reflected in the mirror each is to the other. It's a slow, delight-filled vertigo prolonging the laceration of the flesh. The face of the beloved draws its poignant nature, its insane enticement from this.

The more inaccessible the object of desire, the more it communicates a feeling of vertigo. The greatest vertigo comes from the beloved's uniqueness.

The vertigo of what is unique isn't a simple feeling of vertigo but joy multiplied by vertigo that can't be borne. Of course, in the end individuality (uniqueness) is lost, emptiness is everything, and joy is changed to distress (love dies, unable to pass beyond either uniqueness or joy). But beyond the destruction of the unique begin different uniquenesses. Beyond joy changed to distress, new beings change new feelings of vertigo into joy.

Isolate being is a deception (which reflects the crowd's distress by reversing it), and the couple, becoming stable at last, is a negation of love. But what goes from one lover to the other is a movement that puts an end to isolation or at least makes it waver. Isolate being is *risked*, opens to what's beyond itself, to what's beyond the couple even—monstrous excess.

8

Now I want to talk about myself. I've, myself, taken the same paths I've shown to you.

How can I describe the anguish in which I'm sinking? Only exhaustion speaks for me! My face so wholly expressing fear, my mood so depressed, ruin so entirely winning in me, I might as well think of myself as dead already.

Each day trying to think the unthinkable, in debauch after debauch looking for…coming so close to the void I almost die: I walled myself up in my anguish. All the better to be ripped and torn by prostitutes ripping and tearing me. The more I'd experience fear, and the more divine was the message of shame I learned from a prostitute's body.

At last, rear ends of whores appeared surrounded by a halo of spectral light—and I lived in that light.

In order to seek out extremes of possibility in a slit, I was conscious of ruining myself, of going beyond my strength.

Anguish is the same as desire. I've lived wearing myself out with more desires than I can count, and throughout my life, anguish has been a disappointment. As a schoolboy I waited for the bell that meant classes were out, and today I wait for the object of my anguish till I can't stand it. Terror inhabits me, taking possession of me on a pretext. In these moments what I love is death. If I could only escape, evade *this present state*, the loneliness and boredom of a life that confines itself.

Sometimes I'll admit I'm a coward—saying to myself, there are *others* who are more to be pitied since they're not like me, gasping for breath, beating my head against a wall. I get hold of myself and feel ashamed, then discover a second type of cowardice inside of me. Obviously it was cowardly to get worked up *over such trivial things*, but it's also cowardly to run away from anguish, to look for confidence and self-assurance in indifference. At the opposite end of indifference (the fact of suffering *over such trivial things*) begins an *ascent of Carmel* (although it's also appropriate, in the fullness of distress, to stand up to horror and fight back).

There's a harsh law accepted by those with no yearning for the summit, and it's gentle and desirable. But what's needed is going on (as far as you can) because *gentleness will always fail*.

ALLELUIA 159

There's a need I have to undress whores, a compulsive need for a void beyond me where I'll sink in darkness....

9

A child's despair, night, a graveyard, the tree from which they'll make my coffin shaking in a fierce wind: a finger that slides into your secret parts, you all red, your heart thumping and death slowly coming into that heart....

Across the threshold on whose far side reigns silence and fear...in a church-like dark, your rear end the mouth of a god inspiring devil-like gloom in me.

To leave off words, to die slowly. Such is the condition of endless laceration. In this silent expectation, the gentlest touch awakens pleasure. Awaken your mind to the pleasure of indecency! From there, slipping further and further back, into silence, you'll come to understand how the world's shaped in abandonment and death. You'll picture it, and what's veiled in your dress will feel the outcome: all those lucid nudities on the verge of the same abyss experiencing spasms of the same joy, of the same anguish.

You're a target. Why try to run away? Certain capacities are inevitably deceptive. Neither your insincerity nor your irony can substitute for strength. Even if you try to escape it, the slut nature that is now your possibility will find you again. Not that you'd be bound by this pleasure. But you can only go on, open and happy...and up ahead is the worst. Whatever leads beyond the poverty of each passing moment— beyond the gloom transforming your life into death's limit—won't leave you free in your own mind. A return isn't possible, even if you choose it.

Make no mistake. The morality you hear—which is the one I'm teaching—is the most difficult. It won't let you attain either sleep or satisfaction.

What I ask of you is hell's purity. Or if you will, a child's. This purity won't include a promise of reciprocity, and you won't be bound by obligation. *Coming from yourself* you'll hear a voice leading you to your fate. It's the voice of desire, not desirable *persons*.

To be honest, pleasure scarcely matters. It's received as an extra. The pleasure or joy, the demented *alleluia* of fear, is a sign you've reached the point of making your heart vulnerable. In this half-imagined beyond when everything erodes, moist rainy roses grow bright in the light of storms....

Again I see the masked stranger whose anguish disrobed her in the whorehouse. Her face was hidden, her body naked—her coat, dress, lingerie scattered over the carpet.

We use pleasure as a springboard to enter that region of dreams. And surely pleasure isn't found unless conventional arrangements are destroyed and a fearful world is brought into existence. But the converse is just as true. We'd never find the unlucky flood of light that reveals the truth if pleasure didn't support our insupportable steps.

Your business in this world isn't to assure the salvation of a soul anxious for peace. Nor is it to provide your body with the advantages money brings. Your business is questing for an unknowable destiny. Because of this you'll have to struggle by hating limits—limits which the system of respectability sets up against freedom. On account of this, you'll need to arm yourself with secret pride and indomitable willpower. The advantages given to you by chance—your beauty, glamour, and the untamed impulsiveness of your life—are required for your laceration.

Of course this way of accounting for things won't actually be manifest: you could compare the light that emanates from you to the moonlight falling on a sleeping countryside. All the same, the pitiful state of your nakedness and the terror you experience fidgeting in your nakedness, will be enough to destroy the image of humans as having a limited fate. As lightning as it strikes opens truth to anyone it touches, eternal death, revealed in the pleasures of the flesh, will reach the chosen few. These elect will accompany you to a night where all that's human is destroyed. For only a vast dark, hidden from daylight's slavishness, could conceal a light that's so blindingly bright. And so in the *alleluia* of nakedness you aren't yet at a summit where truth is totally revealed. Beyond sick ecstasies you'll still need laughter as you enter into death's shadow. At that moment all bonds linking you to anything solid will break and fall away. I don't know if you'll laugh or cry, discovering your countless sisters in the sky....